The Diary of Madison Brown

S J Crabb

Copyrighted Material

Copyright © S J Crabb 2016

S J Crabb has asserted her rights under the Copyright, Designs and Patents Act 1988 to be identified as the Author of this work.

This book is a work of fiction and except in the case of historical fact, any resemblance to actual persons, living or dead, is purely coincidental.

All rights reserved. No part of this book may be reproduced or transmitted in any form without written permission of the author, except by a reviewer who may quote brief passages for review purposes only.

NB: This book uses UK spelling.

Contents

Prologue
January 1st
Saint Batholomew's Church
Mum's Roast beef
Sales meeting
Motivational Speaker
January 5th
Channel Island's Trip
Guernsey Airport
Harbour Spa & Retreat
January 17th
January 18th
Lockdown Lifted
James's Office
February 5th
Valentine's Day
March 1st
March 11th
Easter Sunday
Crash & Burn
Thames View Apartments
May 2nd

Gatwick Airport
John F Kennedy Airport – New York
Bellini Biscuits
Teddy's Office
The Coffee House
Tommy's Apartment
Tommy's Sister's wedding
Tommy's Apartment
James's House in Dorset
Bellini Biscuits
Parkmead Flat
The day before James's birthday
Parkmead – Esher
15th October
Advertising Awards
Epilogue
Note from Author
Social Links
More Books
My Christmas Boyfriend Preview

More books by S J Crabb

The Diary of Madison Brown
My Perfect Life at Cornish Cottage
My Christmas Boyfriend
Jetsetters
More from Life
A Special Kind of Advent
Fooling in love
Will You

sjcrabb.com

Prologue

The music is extremely loud and there are more sweaty people jumping around than in a Gymathon! I can't find Ginge, typical! She is always going missing and I spend most of my time looking for her.

It's not as though she ever worries about where I am. After all, she knows I'm the sensible one and do enough worrying for the both of us.

I push my way through the heaving mass of sweaty bodies, trying not to touch anyone on the way. At last, I think I see her; she is dancing on some sort of stage thing, ever the exhibitionist.

"Ginge!" I shout, trying to catch her eye.

"Ginge!"

"There's no need to be rude," says an irate voice in my left ear.

I turn quickly to see a flame-haired young man, about 18 I guess, glaring at me. He says angrily.

"If you want to get past, you only have to say excuse me."

Before I can even reply he storms off. Oh, for goodness' sake, some people are so sensitive; I didn't even know he was there.

Frantically I start waving to grab her attention. All around me people are dancing and singing and are, let's face it, drunk as skunks. Although why they are referred to as such is beyond me; I mean I've never actually seen a drunk skunk, have you?

Ginge is my best friend and flatmate. She is not actually ginger, more a platinum blonde, with the disgusting looks and figure of a supermodel. Her nickname comes from the fact that she is called, Virginia Becton-Smythe. It got shortened to Ginge at school and has stuck ever since; in fact, only her family call her Virginia.

We've been friends since school and live together in Parkmead - the new development of starter homes and flats in Esher. Ginge's parents bought her one for her 18th birthday - luckily, they are loaded and couldn't wait to off-load her to her own space. It was probably cheaper than the cleaning bill as she is not exactly the perfect housewife.

I live there rent-free in return for doing the housekeeping.

Ginge is an Air Stewardess and spends most of her time on trips abroad, so it's like living on my own, really.

No such glamour for me. I'm a beleaguered sales rep for Scentastic, a company which sells home scented products.

"Ginge!" I shout again and she suddenly sees me and waves. Cupping her hands to her mouth she shouts, "I'm coming down!"

Shocked, I watch as she leaps from the stage thing like a gazelle, gracefully flying through the air and landing beside me with a big grin on her face. Wow! If I did that, I would probably break a leg or something.

She shouts in my ear. "Come on Maddie, let's get a drink!"

She pushes me through the sweaty throng, using me like a battering ram, until we get to the bar.

"Two J20's!" she shouts to the bartender who has miraculously become available, despite the crowd nearby vying for his attention.

Ginge has that effect on men. They fall down before her like worshippers at the feet of Aphrodite.

"Are you having fun?" she shouts. I just nod, words are difficult in this environment.

We grab our drinks and find a seat nearby in a green leather clad booth. "God, I'm knackered!" she shouts to me. "I knew I should have gone to bed after the flight, but then it is New Year's Eve, after all, I can sleep tomorrow."Just then - it's never long - two guys slide into the booth beside us. They look like Insurance salesmen, whatever they are supposed to look like."Hey girls, fancy a drink?" Insurance salesman no1 says to Ginge. She flutters her eyelashes at him - oh here we go, I think with exasperation. She is such a tease. Ginge loves nothing more than toying with the opposite sex, as part of some elaborate game, that she concocts on our nights out. Not that they stand a chance with her as she has a boyfriend. Not just any old boyfriend either; he's only Rock God, Tommy Carzola, from the Rock band, Crash & Burn. They met when the band flew first class on the airline she works for. It was lust at first sight for them both and she arranges her work trips around wherever he is in the world on tour. She's just returned from Japan where they are currently touring.

"Thanks, we'll have another couple of J20s." She says smiling sweetly at him. He almost runs off to get them and she turns her attention to his friend. "Hi," she says lowering her eyelashes.

"My name is Amanda, and this is Fiona."

The lad coughs nervously and manages to croak out, "Ian and my friend is Stewart."

"What do you do Ian?" she says slowly and huskily.

He turns bright red and luckily for him, Stewart arrives back with the drinks. He almost spills them in his haste to sit down and I smile at him, trying to put him at ease.

Ginge picks up the drink and placing the straw suggestively in her mouth, proceeds to suck the orange liquid up.

Ian and Stew look at her, almost panting like puppy dogs.

"So, what do you boys do for a living?" she asks them, running her tongue suggestively around her lips.

"We work at Accisurance." Stew manages to stutter out while staring at her in total disbelief.

I flash Ginge a triumphant look, I knew it! I can tell an Insurance person a mile off.

"What about you?" Stew stutters out looking disbelievingly at his friend.

"Well, we are set designers for Downton Abbey."

Ginge says without missing a beat.

This scenario is typical on our nights out. We have been many names with many jobs, from croupiers to film extras. I was an airline pilot once which was cool and Ginge's favourite is a character at a theme park. She's been everything from Pocahontas to Minnie Mouse.

They look impressed, and she is just about to launch into the full screenplay when the music stops. The DJ announces that it will soon be midnight and calls for everyone to take their places ready for the countdown.

"Sorry Guys, must dash," says Ginge pulling me along with her like two modern days Cinderellas.

We rush onto the dance floor, link arms and count down with the crowd.

3-2-1 - HAPPY NEW YEAR!!!

We hug each other and anyone else near us and all link arms for Auld Lang Syne. I notice the Insurance salesmen trying to break through the crowd, but they don't stand a chance - luckily!

I look around and then at my best friend. I love her to bits and feel so lucky that we have such a good life together. Maybe this is my year; I will find the man of my dreams, get the promotion at work and become the person that I want to be.

Now all I need is a plan.

January 1st - New Year's Day

I woke up fairly early despite the late night. Ginge is still sleeping and probably will be until tomorrow. She has been known to sleep for 16 hours after a trip - especially one involving Tommy.

Ok, today is the first day of mission life plan. There is no time to waste. I must make this year count and need to know how to achieve my desires. First things first- Resolutions.

I grab my new notebook, the one that says Random Crap and set about compiling my list.

1: Work hard and achieve promotion.

2: Save money and don't impulse buy.

3: Phone home at least every other day - not once a fortnight after a drunken night out.

4: Be organised at work and at home.

5: Be kind to everyone - even Cardigan Darren!

6: Find everlasting love.

Ok, now I'm stuck. How exactly do people achieve their lifelong ambitions when they don't actually know what they are?

The phone vibrates and I can see it is Mum. I groan

inwardly. Oh, no am I ready for this so soon in the year? I answer the phone and whisper, "Hi Mum, I can't talk loudly, Ginge is still sleeping."

Mum just shouts, "Happy New Year Madison, will we be seeing you this year, I mean we haven't seen you since last year?"

Mum goes off into peals of laughter; she says the same thing every year and still thinks it's hilarious.

"Are you doing your New Year's Day Roast Beef?" I ask hopefully. Mum and Dad don't live far so it wouldn't take me long to nip around for a hearty New Year's meal. "Yes of course we are, it's traditional."

Happily, I say, "Ok I'll be round about 2 pm. Ginge probably won't make it though as we'll be lucky to see her at all today."

"Ok dear, see you soon - love you Bunny Boo."

Oh, my God I wish she would stop calling me "Bunny Boo." She thinks that it's her mission in life to embarrass me at every opportunity.

After I hang up, I take stock of the situation.

Hmm, it's 10 am. 4 hours to go until lunch. Maybe I should get dressed for the occasion. As I look down at my pink pyjamas with the pandas on, I think I better had.

Right! New Year new me.

As I sift through my wardrobe, I can't believe how many clothes I have that I never wear. Ok, the first rule of the year, wear something different every day until you have worn everything - or chuck it out.

That thought fills me with dread. I am a terrible hoarder and won't throw anything away. I still have my old school uniform from Primary School - of course, it doesn't fit anymore, but it has sentimental memories. Actually, I hated school and school hated me why do I want to remember it?

Spying some really cool leather look trousers, that I had to have after watching Easy Rider, I decide on those with a leopard print top and a fur-trimmed jacket. Fake of course, nothing is real in my life after all.

Great, I look like a cool rock chick. Although I am not sure why I bought any of this really, it was probably after Ginge started seeing Tommy; we went to one of their concerts so I wanted to fit in. Jeans would have done though- never mind they can be my new look.

I rummage through the shoe boxes under my bed. Dusting off a large box, I open it and reveal the leopard print boots that I bought and never wore, probably because they have heels. I'm a flats girl, really.

Right, I had better not eat any breakfast otherwise I won't be hungry for lunch. I look at my watch and notice there are still three hours before I have to leave.

Ok, I'm bored already. I wish that Ginge would wake up. We could have a laugh and watch an old movie, Grease would be good, as I am embracing my inner Sandy.

Suddenly the doorbell rings sending me into a state of panic. Oh, my God, don't wake up Ginge!

I scurry to the door, fling it open and groan inwardly.

Cardigan Darren, our next-door neighbour is standing there trying to look cool and failing miserably. He has a very obvious crush on me, which I definitely do not reciprocate. He has sensible brown hair and glasses and always wears a cardigan - even in the summer - and is the most stylishly challenged person that I have ever met.

He looks at me nervously and plays with his fingers, which he always does when he wants something. His eyes widen as he takes in my outfit, hah, he has noticed the new me, I think with a sense of achievement.

"Sorry Darren," I whisper, "I can't invite you in because Ginge is asleep. Happy New Year by the way."

he flashes a brief smile. "Happy New Year Maddie."

Once again, he licks his lips nervously. Inwardly I

roll my eyes. Oh, for goodness' sake spit it out I haven't got all year.

Then I remember my New Year's resolution to be kind to him, so I say gently.

"How can I help you, Darren, do you need to borrow anything?"

He blushes. "Only you, if you don't mind?"

Ok, this is odd but hear him out before giving in to the urge to run inside and bolt the door. "Mind what?" I say encouragingly.

"Well, it's the Love thy neighbour service at Church today and we have been asked to invite our neighbours to come with us."

He must have seen the abject horror on my face because he carries on quickly. "Please say you will come? It won't take long and I'll buy you a coffee afterwards to say thank you."

Now normally, I would do most things for a free Latte, as I'm kind of addicted, but Church!!

He is looking so hopefully at me that I can't refuse; it would be like kicking a puppy dog.

"Ok." I sigh resigned to my fate, maybe I might receive divine inspiration for my new life!

"When is it?"

"In half an hour, actually so we should leave now, if you are ready," he says looking a bit worried at my would-be Church outfit.

I smile inside, my inner Devil coming out, apt for where we are heading. I can't wait to see the Vicar's face when I rock up!

11am - Saint Bartholomew's Cof E Church

Well, we are finally here, walking up the gravel path towards enlightenment. Darren had wanted us to cycle here! I mean is he mad. Did he not see my footwear?

I had to put my leopard print foot firmly down; I mean the only way I could cycle here, would be on Ginge's pink Pashley, with a basket in the front. Hardly rock-and-roll.

I told him very firmly that we would be arriving in my company car- well sort of; mine is in having some dents knocked out of it that some idiot gave me in the supermarket car park. He lost control of his trolley and it smashed into the side of my car.

Well, I went off my trolley too, until I realised that he was actually quite gorgeous and gave me his number, for Insurance purposes only of course.

Well, I'm due to meet him for a drink to discuss the accident tomorrow evening. Oh well, every cloud and all that.

I am driving the garage courtesy car. It is a VW beetle with, "VW Forestford, for all your servicing needs," emblazoned on the side. It has a really cool flower in a vase inside, so I'm thinking of keeping it.

Darren keeps on trying to hold on to me as we walk up the path. He's probably pretending we're on a date - God forbid. Oh, are you allowed to say that in the shadow of God's house? Actually, you probably are as I'm sure his name is bandied around several times a day here.

The church is really old and imposing. They really should make them more welcoming; I don't know maybe like a Costa or something, with little tables and chairs outside, under church logo related umbrellas. They could serve up their messages on the side of small, medium, or large, coffee cups. I'm sure they would be inundated by customers then and would probably make a profit.

I see the Vicar ahead of us, resplendent in his white billowing gown. He looks a jolly sort. I might pitch my idea to him later; failing that, he may need some scented candles for the vestry, they always smell musty. I bet women Vicars allocate a large part of their budget to scented candles and diffusers.

Note to self - pitch idea of selling to Churches at next Sales Meeting.

Seeing us approaching a broad smile breaks out over the Vicar's face and Darren grabs hold of my hand.

I knew it the sly little cardigan wearing weasel; it was all a ploy to get me on a date. Well, 1/10 for the venue.

Not wishing to embarrass him in front of his idol I leave it in place, but stiffen my lips to indicate my disapproval.

"You must be Maddie," says the Vicar beaming at me; although looking a bit bewildered as he takes in my attire. God! -sorry- he even knows my name. Do they have confessionals here, what has Darren been saying about me?!

I smile at him warmly.

"Good morning, I'm pleased to meet you - my neighbour Darren has told me nothing about you."

Actually, I didn't say that last bit, I just wanted to.

"Well, I'm pleased that you could make it at last. Darren has told us lots about you and how your busy life keeps you away a lot. Never mind, you've made it at last. We can have a nice jolly chat after the service."

What!!! I look at Darren incredulously. He blushes a deep shade of red and won't look me in the eye.

Snatching my hand away I go to speak but we are interrupted by a young woman heading purposefully towards us.

She is very slight and pale, with shoulder-length brown hair which is held back by an Alice band. Oh, my God - sorry- she is also wearing a cardigan.

This is the cardigan club if ever I saw one.

She doesn't look very happy and stands in front of us with a blank expression on her face.

"Hello Darren, who's your friend?" she says, with no trace of emotion or spark in her voice at all.

Maybe she's a robot. She is looking at me, actually no, she is staring at me in the most unfriendly manner.

Darren shifts anxiously on his feet looking at me pleadingly and I suddenly totally get the situation.

Miss Cardigan obviously has her sights set on Mr Cardigan here and for whatever reason he has, he has used me to put her off. Ok, now I understand, it's time to put my game face on, for my friend.

Grabbing Darren's hand, I pull him beside me.

"Oh Hi, my name is Maddie," I say in my best Ginge voice.

"I'm Darren's very good friend and we practically live together."

Well, we do as only a wall separates our flats.

Oh God - sorry- I just realise that I am committing a sin in the presence of God; in his house, actually. Well, it's for a good cause namely Cardigan Darren.

He shoots me a very grateful look, which is the total opposite to the one she shoots me. He quickly pulls me down the aisle towards a pew near the front, shoving me along quickly, before the organ starts playing.

Looking around, I notice there are quite a few people here. I'm surprised we are so near the front. There aren't many more seats; although Miss Cardigan manages to find one on the end of our row. She glowers at me as the organ plays, its dour melody perfectly reflecting my mood.

God - sorry- it's cold in here. They really should get some heaters, maybe under pew heating. I'm sure that would make more people want to come.

Mental Note: Pitch under pew heating idea to Vicar during jolly chat.

The Vicar takes his place and starts droning on about friendship and the importance of neighbours. The only importance of neighbours in our house relates to the television programme. It's on Sky Plus and we have regular neighbourthons, involving back-to-back episodes, accompanied by huge Toblerones.

Why are Churches so boring? They could be such fun if they just thought about it. They could have songs and videos; with films, such as The Da Vinci Code and Raiders of the Lost Ark. They could replace the pews, with comfy settees, with little coffee tables. Oh, my God - sorry- the list is endless.

I could become a consultant for the Church Body and I would be single-handedly responsible for the Christianity craze that would sweep the land.

I smile happily to myself at the thought but then I'm aware of Darren nudging me. I quickly beam back to earth, just in time to hear the Vicar calling my name.

"Maddie, come on up and say a few words about Darren and what it means to be a good neighbour."

Everyone starts clapping and I look at Darren in confusion. Whoa, what did I miss?

Darren looks at me sheepishly and I realise I've been well and truly set up.

I glower at him, but then part of me admires his nerve. He knows I would have never come in a month of Sundays if he had told me. Well hats off to him; although I'll have my revenge and it will be sweet.

I have to push past Miss Cardigan who smirks at me; probably hoping I'll make a complete fool of myself.

Ok! Time for full Oscar-winning drama performance.

I smile sweetly at her as I turn to face the smiling Vicar. As I pass him I dazzle him with my full beam and head up to the pulpit.

I look around, pretending that I'm picking up an award, at some ceremony on another and smile happily at everyone. I can see Darren squirming in his seat. Oh yes, squirm away little Judas, you have every reason to be afraid.

I touch the microphone to test it's on, in true Hollywood style. In fact, I must be quite a sight in my Rock Rebel outfit, with crazy hair. I haven't mentioned my hair yet. Well, there's me and then there's my hair. It's a crazy blonde afro of the tightest corkscrew curls, that hovers around my head, defying even the most sophisticated straighteners on the market. I normally wear it tied up in some desperate act to control it, but today it is down and flying around me, in all its glory.

Looking out in front of me I see the sea of faces, waiting to hear what I have to say. I've never been good at public speaking, but I am used to speaking to strangers - after all, I sell for a living. Ok here goes!

"Hi everyone, my name's Maddie and I'm Darren's neighbour and friend. Stand up Darren and give everyone a wave."

Darren looks at me with a mortified expression.

Revenge Step No 1: public humiliation.

He stands up quickly, waves and then hurriedly sits down. Oh no you don't treacherous neighbour. "Come up here Darren, with me." I shout at him. He shakes his head, a look of horror on his face. Ha, two can play at this game matey.

I wait, saying nothing until resigned to his fate he shuffles his way out of the pew and joins me in the pulpit. Everyone claps and I link arms with him - mainly to annoy Miss Cardigan who is glowering at me.

"Well, Darren is a great friend to have, nothing is too much trouble. I am always locking myself out so Darren comes to my rescue with the spare key that I have entrusted to him." Everyone claps. Ok now for step 2.

Revenge Step No 2: Embarrassment

"Darren selflessly gets my food shopping every week, by bringing home £20 worth of past their sell by date food and beverage items. Without his generosity, I wouldn't eat as well as I do."

The congregation looks aghast, but this bit is actually true. The food is fine and only just out of date. It's always in its, Best before date, though. We haven't had food poisoning yet, so it must be ok. It saves us a fortune as well as the dreaded weekly shopping trip.

Ok, time to redeem myself with God; after all I mustn't break New Year's Resolution, No 5, on the first day.

I turn to Darren and throw my arms around his neck. He looks afraid and awkward and I feel a sudden rush of love for him. He may be strange, but he's still a great guy and totally deserves what will come next.

"Thanks, Darren, you're the best neighbour I could ever wish for. There's probably not a person here who doesn't wish you were their neighbour. I'm the luckiest girl in the world."

Then I plant a massive smacker on his bemused cheek.

The Vicar coughs, Darren now resembles a beetroot and Miss Cardigan looks as if she's been sprayed by a skunk. Why is everything always about skunks? Do we even have them in this country?

However, the rest of the congregation give him a huge clap. Some even offer a standing ovation. Maybe he will become the legend of, St Bartholomew's and it's all thanks to me and my overactive imagination.

We descend the pulpit victorious and once again push our way back into the pew.

The rest of the sermon is as boring as the first part; I call them the BM and PM periods. Before Madison and Post Madison.

Looking at my watch, I notice that it's already 1.30pm. God -sorry, when will I learn? - Mum's Roast Beef!

2.30pm - Mum's Traditional New Year's Day Roast Beef.

Well, I managed to get out of the Church without further incident. I had to promise Reggie, The Vicar, a rain check on our Jolly chat and left Cardigan Darren amid a throng of interested women to make my way to mum's for lunch.

She is in fine form even though Dad looks a little worse for wear. Apparently, they spent the evening at, Elvis Chan's Chinese New Year Restaurant; Dad has to drink large amounts of alcohol to survive a night out with my mother. The lunch is sublime though. I always love my Mother's cooking and need at least an hour sleep afterwards before I can think about moving. I'm still a bit annoyed at her though as she doesn't think Rock Rebel is the sort of new image that I should be sporting. What does she know about fashion, anyway? She thinks that Mary Berry's a fashion icon.

"So, Bunny Boo, tell me your New Year's resolutions. Do they involve looking for a husband? After all, I was married by your age."

"Mum! Please don't wish marriage on me at 25, most people now wait until they are at least 30 before they settle down. It's all about the experiences at my age." "You've been experiencing things for far too long, in my opinion, how about experiencing married life and babies?"

I will never win this argument with mum. I think she's just jealous that she didn't have as many experiences as I do so she's trying to curb my enjoyment.

Time to go, I think. I have a sales meeting planned first thing in the morning and I have to drive for 2 hours to get there. It was obviously planned by someone who doesn't experience the joys of New Year!

6.00pm Packing for Sales Meeting

Ginge is still out cold so I am tiptoeing around the flat trying to get organised for tomorrow. I have to leave at 6.30am to get to the sales meeting by 9.00am. I hope that the courtesy car is up to a long journey!

If I leave my clothes out ready, I can get a bit more sleep. Now, what shall I wear? It has to say successful business professional at the top of her game. There must be something like that in here. I pull out a navy suit. Hmm, this may do - oh no I've remembered I wore that at the last trade show, it has to be something they've never seen before. What about that smart black shift dress with a green jacket? No, I think I wore that to the last sales meeting. The trouble is most of the time I wear quite casual clothes to work that say to my customers - non-confrontational, easy going, no pressure rep come to have a chat and you can buy something if you want sort of thing.

I know, what about that pink tunic with leggings and knee-length boots? I can wear a smart jacket and my attitude glasses. That's it, I will look every inch the successful salesperson- and they have never seen me wear it! Right, job done. Now I just need to look up the address on multimap - the courtesy car doesn't have sat nav - and I will be ready.

7.00pm Box set of Desperate Housewives/ selection box from Auntie Maureen

Ginge woke up so we decided on a marathon box set evening with snacks. Aunty Maureen always buys me a selection box - "You're never too old for these love," - she always says, a wise woman my Aunt. We love just sitting in our pyjamas tucking into chocolate and absorbing the lives of people that we aspire to be.

10.00pm - Disc 3

12.00pm - Bed!!!

January 2nd - Scentatstic Sales Meeting

6.30am! Oh, no I should be leaving by now and I've just woken up! I'll just quickly grab everything and get dressed on the way. Luckily New Year's resolution no 3 helped me to be organised so I can just throw it all in and dress in the car.

7.30am!!! Gridlock on the M25. Everybody is back to work today it seems at the same time.

8.00am - Driven 3 junctions. Haven't even been able to change out of pink panda pyjamas because an artic lorry is next to me and the driver keeps on looking at me and smiling.

8.10am - Lorry driver into sign language. I pretend I don't understand; why won't this traffic move?

8.20am - phone Matty my colleague from work. Have my headphones on so hands-free.

"Hi, Maddie, are you here yet?"

"What do you mean here, are you there already?"

"Yes, they've even laid on bacon rolls - Betty has got the caterers in, it all looks really impressive. Where are you then?"

"M25, at least half an hour away."

"Never mind, Happy New Year by the way."

"Yes, you too. How are the twins?" Matty and his wife have twin boys, Lucas and Ephesus, I know, I blame celebrities for this weird name trend.

"Nightmare! Jemima's stupid bitch mother gave them each a drum for Christmas, another punishment present."

Matty's mother-in-law has never forgiven them for not calling the boys, George and Derek, after her father and husband. She keeps on finding little ways to punish them for defying her wishes. The boys are only 3 years old and shall we say a little challenging in the behaviour department.

"Yes, it's been one hell of a Christmas. I got here at 7 am just to get out of the house. I told Jemima that we had to stay over and have booked the Premier Inn for a night of alone time, just me and the TV, with a few beers for company and possibly a pizza - heaven!"

I laugh out loud; Matty always cheers me up even in the most stressful of situations.

"Oh, my God, there's a space with my name on it. Matty, stall the meeting for as long as you can, I'm finally on my way."

Isn't it unbelievable how traffic just melts away all of a sudden with no reason for the hold-up? One of life's mysteries.

9.10 am

Right, I'm here! Just got to get changed and then I can head inside looking every inch the successful salesperson that I am. Well, I would have been if Scent City hadn't gone bankrupt last year and cost us thousands of pounds in unpaid bills. My figures fell like a bungee jumper and I went from being top of the pyramid to the bottom in one fell swoop.

9.20am

I CAN'T FIND MY LEGGINGS!!!

I am sure that they were with the rest of the clothes. Think think! Oh no, I remember now, Ginge was cold and Mike had just got shot in Desperate Housewives, she grabbed my leggings so that she didn't have to pause it. Knowing her, she is probably still wearing them!

Ok, don't panic. Just keep your coat on and you'll be fine.

So, I exit the car dressed in a pink tunic that barely covers my best Primanis, with knee-high boots and a flasher mac. At least I have my Attitude glasses to pull the look together. Luckily, I have a scrunchie for my hair. Good to go.

"Where have you been, you're late?"

Oh, no it's Betty Bulldog, and she looks really cross. Betty is really called, Elizabeth Bailey, and she is my Sales Manager. We call her Betty Bulldog because she looks like one and has a thin angry mouth that looks like she has swallowed a wasp. She is quite scary really and rules over us with a rod of iron. "Sorry Elizabeth didn't Matty tell you, the M25 was gridlocked."

"No, he didn't," she says crossly. "He was probably too busy polishing off the bacon rolls."

At the mention of these, I look around hopefully. I am starving and the breakfast bar that I ate in the car is a distant memory.

"Well you're too late to eat anything now as we are just about to start," she snaps.

"We have to get a move on because our guest speaker will be here at 11.00am along with the rest of the company."

I groan inwardly while maintaining a look of feigned interest. Betty loves her motivational speeches. At least if it's someone else we will be spared her attempts. Last time it was all about "Raising the Bar." By the end of it, the only bar I wanted to raise was the one above her head before I knocked her out with it.

Note to self - Try to stop having murderous thoughts towards your Boss, not healthy!

"Anyway, you can put your coat over there and then we had better start."

Oh no, this is staying on me, for one it's freezing in here and I don't intend on flashing my best Primanis to my colleagues until I have at least had a few drinks. "Oh, that's ok, I'll keep it on until I've warmed up a bit if that's alright?"

Raising her eyes up she ushers me into the room.

There are about 12 of us Sales Reps and I actually like all of them - unusual in this day of competition but we all get along great, united in our common hatred of Betty. I can see them grinning at me and I grin back like a naughty schoolgirl. Now I know why they look so pleased with themselves, the last empty seat is the one next to Betty. Oh well, I don't blame them. I blow kisses around the room and head into the fray.

God, I'm so bored! Betty's been droning on about sales growth and opportunities for the last hour and it's really difficult to maintain an interested expression for this long, especially on nothing more than a breakfast bar.

Matty has fallen asleep. She can't see him because having been the first to arrive he bagged the seat on the end facing away from Betty. Oh well, he probably needs to catch up with some sleep after living in toddler hell over Christmas. Oh no, she is moving to the flip chart, this looks like trouble.

"Now, I have posted up your sales positions on the pyramid. Well done Robert, you have achieved first place position. Maybe you could let the Team know your secret so that they too can reach the dizzy heights of No1 salesperson."

We all clap and Robert looks around grinning. "What's my prize?" he says cheekily and Betty answers,

"It is being secure in the knowledge that you have a job for another year," she says looking hard at me as she says it.

I can see my name on the chart residing firmly at the bottom of the pyramid. When I say pyramid, it is more like a block of flats, really. I am firmly in the basement flat position which isn't fair. I am normally in the Penthouse position and it's only because Scent City went bust that I have plummeted so far down. Everyone knows it but Betty can't resist digging the knife in.

"Madison, we must have a talk about the opportunities in your area after your disastrous year, so please stay behind while the others head outside for coffee and biscuits while we wait for the rest to join us."

She is now officially the Devil Incarnate. She knows that I haven't eaten and could murder a coffee. I look over at Matty in alarm and he reassures me via sign language that he will get me a coffee and biscuits. I do love Matty, he always knows what I'm thinking even before I think it sometimes. As they leave Betty points to my position on the board and circles it with a big red marker pen. "Doesn't look good, does it, Madison?" I shake my head but think; I'm not having this it isn't my fault. Before I can even speak, she rants on.

"You can't just blame Scent City for this, it is your job as a salesperson to anticipate potential problems and plan accordingly. Everyone loses accounts at some time or another but you have to have others waiting in the wings to take up the slack when they fail. I am disappointed that you didn't plan for this so I want you to go away and look for any potential that can replace this account. Now I must go as the guest speaker has probably arrived and you probably want a drink - oh and lose the coat it's not Siberia in here."

I watch her click away in her four-inch heels. She can only be 5ft so she wears these huge heels to give her an advantage. The trouble is she is so round that it looks ridiculous.

Heading outside I see Matty waiting with the nectar of the God's that is a coffee with some gorgeous looking biscuits.

"Thought you could do with this, oh and I pinched a plate full of biscuits. Here I put them in this carrier bag, they will keep us going through the next hour or so of motivation."

"Thanks, Matty, you know that you're my favourite don't you?"

I grin at him. Suddenly with horror, I realise that the whole company is turning up for the speaker and Betty has left the Flip chart in full view of everyone, with my name circled in red at the bottom.

"Hold this for me Matty; I have to do something before everyone goes in."

Quickly I race back into the room. I'll just flip over the page and no one will know. Why are these things so awkward? I grab hold of the sheet and try to throw it over the top of the board but it is so tall and keeps on falling back down. Maybe if I jump up at the same time. No, it's not working and I haven't got long. Grabbing a nearby chair I stand on it to get height advantage just as Betty and her guest enter the room.

"Madison! What on earth are you doing?"

Startled I look around and the chair wobbles precariously. Reaching out to steady myself I fall against the Flip chart and it rocks dangerously. The guest speaker races over and grasps hold of me and then lifts me down in one Super Hero move. How embarrassing!

I look up at my rescuer who can't be much older than me and is looking at me with an amused expression on his rather handsome face. Betty, however, is most definitely not amused.

"Madison, what on earth are you playing at? Actually, no don't tell me, I haven't got the time. Please, for the last time, take your coat off and then take a seat. I suggest that you listen very carefully for the next hour because you of all people will benefit most from it."

Hero Man looks at me, a smile threatening to break out but concealing it rather well in my opinion.

Matty comes in at that point and seeing him Betty says, "Give Matty your coat, he knows where they go."

Oh, no I can't. "I'm still a bit cold; I think I'll keep it on if you don't mind."

"Yes, I do mind, I don't want you fidgeting around taking it off when the temperature goes up once everyone is in the room."

Ok, you've asked for this. I slowly take it off and watch with great delight the horror that unfolds on Betty's face as she takes in my lack of leggings. The tunic literally just covers my bottom and with the knee-high boots I look like a hooker.

Matty snorts involuntarily and rather skilfully turns it into a cough. Hero man looks really surprised but Betty's face is like thunder.

"Did you forget something?" she says now apoplectic.

"Sorry, I think my flatmate is wearing my leggings. I drove here in my pyjamas so didn't know until it was too late."

This time Hero Man has to look away and I can see his shoulders shaking. "Put the coat back on and sit down. I will speak to you later," says Betty wearily, before turning to her guest and feigning a smile.

"I am so sorry James, what on earth must you think of us. Come; let me get you a coffee and some biscuits while everyone takes their places."

She ushers him out of the room and Matty explodes with laughter.

"Maddie, you are a legend." He laughs uncontrollably.

Laughing I say, "Come on let's sit down, is Big John here?"

"Yes."

"Good, let's wait at the back until he comes in."

Big John, as his name suggests is huge. He is 6ft tall and as wide and he runs the warehouse. He is in such demand on these sorts of occasions if you wish to hide as his frame obscures at least three people's view. Not the person you want in front of you in the theatre or cinema, but perfect for sales meetings.

"He's coming," whispers Matty and we look for where he is going to sit.

The trouble is, so does everybody else and there is usually a mad dash to get behind him first. He looks around and there is silence as everyone places themselves strategically around the room. Suddenly I have a brainwave. "John! Over here, I need to ask you something." The rest of the room look daggers at me.

"He's coming", I whisper excitedly to Matty.

"Hi Maddie, what do you want to know?" he says genuinely believing me.

"Oh, sit in front of me there and I'll tell you, otherwise, the seats will all go."

He looks surprised as of course, nobody has sat down yet. As he lowers his huge frame into the seat in front, Matty and I gloat at the others as we take our seats behind him. He looks around expectantly.

"Sorry John, nothing urgent, I was just wondering if you knew who that guy is talking to Elizabeth?"

"I think that he is the speaker but I don't know where from or what he is going to say."

Just then somebody else sits down beside me and I turn to see Brian Harris, the owner of Scentastic grabbing the third coveted seat behind John.

"Hi Maddie, I didn't know you wore glasses?"

"Just trying them out Brian, are you hiding too?"

He makes a face and laughs. "Yes, it's the best place to be if you ask me. I am sure it will be interesting but I'm not in the mood to contribute today, what about you? Oh, don't tell me, Scent City?"

"Yes, Betty has almost put my name in lights at the bottom of the sales board so I am keeping out of her way."

"Never mind, you win some you lose some."

"Not according to Betty, I should have seen it in my Crystal Ball and made plans." Matty starts handing out the biscuits and we wait for the inevitable.

12.00pm: James Sinclair - Motivational Speaker.

"Hi everybody my name is James Sinclair and I am the Managing Director of JS Public Relations & Marketing." Time to start texting Matty - we do this all the time in meetings, on silent of course.

 Text to Matty

Rubbish name for a business.
I could do better than that.

He drones on about how he started and made his first million by age 5. I can't see much of him due to the obstruction in front of me but his voice is quite sexy.

"I like to help others learn what the secret is to achieving high sales and win contracts. It is my way of giving something back."

Brian snorts beside me. "More like us giving him £5000 an hour for his secret!"

Wow, that's a serious hourly rate, I am impressed.

"All you need to do is to find out who is the top-selling salesperson in your field and ask them how they do it. Then you do what they do and you will have the same results."

Ask Robert?? I already know his secret. His uncle opened a chain of home stores and buys all his scented products from Rob. Not exactly cutting-edge sales. It's as I always say, it's not what you know but who you know.

"Successful people in life are no different from anybody else. All they have recognised is that they join the queue at the back and stay in line until they reach the front."

Text from Matty

What!!!

"There is one saying that has been found out to be true by asking many successful people over time what it is they think about. The successful ones think of nothing else but their dreams and how they can make them happen. So, it has borne out that, you become what you think about most of the time."

Text to Matty

Ok that makes me a homicidal,

Sex maniac with a shopping

Problem

Text from Matty

That makes me dead!

all I think about is sleep

"As soon as your customers start seeing you as consultants and not sales people then they will treat you differently. You will become their friend and they will trust your judgement. You just need to tell them that you have not come to sell them anything today but you can help advise them of a better way."

Text from Brian

Don't go anywhere and
not sell them anything!!!

One Hour Later:

"So, to wrap up remember - You become what you think about most of the time."

Thank you, everybody. Now I will go around the room and ask for just one word to sum up your experience today."

Text from Matty:

Tosser!

One by one he asks each person in turn. It seems that as soon as I have thought of a word somebody else uses it. Betty is positively having an orgasm in the front, crossing and uncrossing her legs and fluttering her eyelashes at him - gross! Dismiss that word from your mind this instant, I tell myself sternly. Suddenly it's my turn. I still can't see him and I say, "Exciting." Matty and Brian giggle beside me, why did I say that? I meant to say, Informative, what on earth was exciting about it?

Matty says, Informative and I nudge him in the ribs.

Betty stands up and thanks Tosser and then we can all go out for some lunch, hurray, at last, the biscuits lasted 5 minutes and I'm starving!

1.00pm - Lunch

Lunch is quite good for a change and I help myself to sandwiches, cakes, fruit and an orange juice. Chloe, one of the other Reps -sorry consultants - comes over. "Hi Maddie, great to see you, gosh did you see that speaker James! Talk about hot and cool at the same time. Top to toe Ralph Lauren, just how I like them."

"Can't say I noticed him," I say speaking with my mouth full, but I am so hungry I can't eat fast enough.

"I'm not surprised, I saw you engineer the chair behind Big John. Genius. Oh, my God, he's coming over!" she squeals.

Oh no, I just want to stuff my face, not make polite conversation with Tosser.

"Hello Ladies, I am pleased to meet you," he says holding out his hand and Chloe grabs it quickly, the trouble is she is having trouble letting it go. He pulls it away and turns to me.

"Hello - again."

I smile at him noticing that his eyes crinkle up at the corners when he speaks. Actually, he is good looking; his hair is dark and styled in quite a trendy way. He has deep blue eyes and looks tanned and healthy.

"Madison, isn't it?" he says smiling at me and strangely I feel a shiver run through me at the sound of my name on his lips. Chloe is looking at us with a knowing expression. This is confusing, how did I miss how gorgeous this guy really is?

Annoyed with myself for not having spent the last hour staring lustfully at him, instead of looking at Big John's substantial frame, I pull myself together and say, "Yes, I am pleased to meet you, James," and hold out my hand as an excuse to touch him.

As we shake hands my insides melt and I am sure that it must be so obvious to him. I feel like a swooning maiden of yonder years, I am Elizabeth to his Mr Darcy, Cathy to his Heathcliff. "Madison, what area do you cover?"

What?? Oh yes, he is now speaking to me, concentrate. "Oh, mainly the South East of England and the Channel Islands."

"Really, that's interesting. Do you have much in the Channel Islands?"

"Not really because I don't get to spend much time

there. I am going soon though and may book an extra day to look for potential accounts."

He looks thoughtful, his face looks even more handsome in thought and I am so resisting the urge to reach out and touch it. Down Girl!

"I might be able to help you out there; I have an account with Simpson's the large Department Store chain. Do you supply them?"

"No, I have tried several times, but the buyer isn't interested."

"Well, I could put a good word in for you with the owner, Mr Simpson. He owes me a favour." He grins at me and I am lost forever.

"Are you sure? I mean I don't want to put you out."

"Not at all. Give me your phone and I'll put my number in and you can do the same on mine."

Oh, my God, I'm swapping phones with the now re-named MMM (Mr Motivational Man). Chloe has turned green.

While we are typing away, she says,

"Oh Maddie, don't you have a date tonight with Trolley man?"

Bitch! Actually, I forgot about him. MMM looks up and I note with satisfaction the sudden alarm on his face.

"Trolley Man?"

"Yes, his trolley ran into the side of my car in the

supermarket car park and we are meeting up to discuss the accident."

"I don't like the sound of that." MMM says to my surprise, why should he care?

"Oh, it's ok, he's a Fireman or something, isn't that right, Maddie?"

Damn Chloe, why do I spend endless hours while driving, on the phone to her divulging all my secrets?

"Are you sure? It's just that I have heard of so many scams that take place in supermarket car parks. This could be another one. He may not really be a Fireman and could be a murderer or rapist."

Mm, good point, although a tad overdramatic, God could we be any better suited? Oh no, Betty Bulldog approaching, take cover. Chloe spots her and makes a clean getaway. MMM sees her coming and visibly pales. "There you are James, let me rescue you from Madison and introduce you to our leader Brian. Madison, I would like a word with you later so don't run off, I need to arrange your 1-1 as a matter of urgency."

Bitch! Ok, I've now had enough of your sly digs and you've asked for this. I nod and then stare at her without wavering, allowing a slow look of horror to creep over my face. She starts looking around her noticing my expression and looks towards James who is also looking really confused. "Stay still and don't move," I whisper, allowing my voice to change to one of impending doom. She freezes and says, "What is it? what's the matter?"

I whisper loudly for maximum effect, "Spider!"

The result is hilarious, she screams and does the spider dance. Shaking her head and using her fingers she tries to dislodge the imaginary spider. She is still screaming, "Help! Get it off, I hate them!"

I make out as if to help and start batting her around the head with my hands, this is so good, Ginge and I discovered this trick at school and it never fails.

MMM is looking at us incredulously. He is trying and failing to hold it together as the rest of the company look on laughing at the spectacle. Betty runs off in the direction of the Ladies and James and I dissolve into hysterics. "Well Miss Brown, to use your words, it's been exciting," he says when we finally stop. "I agree, Mr Sinclair and may I also add, enlightening."

January 5th

10.30pm

Well, I've been back to work now for 2 days and once again life is normal.

Once the sales meeting had finished, I arrived home and remembered that I had a date that night with Trolley Man. I had been well and truly put off him thanks to MMM and felt a little apprehensive. Never mind, we were meeting in a local Bar so I wouldn't be alone with him and I would take my phone in case of emergencies.

He turned out to be a nice guy. He was a Fireman as previously thought and had me in stitches all night with tales of loose women calling them out to fulfil some sort of sexual fantasy. There were the hilarious anecdotes about children getting their body parts stuck in various household items and the not so good tales of death and destruction.

It doesn't hurt that he is also extremely good looking, in a rugged way and I couldn't take my eyes off of his biceps. He is coming around tomorrow night to fit us with smoke alarms! Strangely mid-way through the evening, I got a text from MMM!

Text from James Sinclair

Miss Brown,

*It was good to meet you
today. I will fwd details of the owner of Simpson's
once called in favour.
Please text back so that I know you are safe,
as expect you are in the meeting.
Regards
James*

Goodness! He remembered my "meeting" this evening and is checking that I am not being murdered by the Supermarket Slayer!

Text to James Sinclair
*It was good to meet you too Mr Sinclair.
Thank you for saving me from a fall and
I would be most grateful for any help with
Simpsons.
You are correct; I am in a meeting which is
progressing well. Thank you for your concern.*

*Regards
Madison
Ps: Make sure you have smoke detectors fitted!*

I don't know why but the text has sort of put a dampener on my evening. Maybe it was the memory of how absolutely gorgeous he was, or the fact that he had taken the time to text me. I felt excitement course through me and as nice as he was, Trolley man just didn't compare.

Ginge is packing for another trip, this time the tour has moved on to Australia - lucky thing. She will be away for 4 days and the flat always seems empty when she is away. We are getting pizza tonight and are thinking of catching up with back-to-back TOWIE.

January 6th - Smoke Alarms installed

Trolley Man-aka Rob came this evening armed with smoke alarms. Cardigan Darren was roped in as chaperone and we had a great night the three of us eating Chinese takeaway and talking about Darren's new hobby - massage. Apparently, he was so inundated with requests from the ladies of the parish to perform his hobby that he decided to enrol on a course. It's taken years off him. I wonder if he will wear a white cardigan with little white shorts as his uniform?

Rob is nice but something is holding me back from agreeing to a second date. I told him that I was away next week and would call him when I get back.

This is true as I have booked my Channel Islands trip, which I am very excited about. I managed to secure a great deal online, given that it's January, for a two-night Gourmet Break at Guernsey's premier hotel. It includes dinner and a separate night at the Michelin star restaurant next door, "Michele's". All for just a little more than the usual B&B.

January 12th - Channel Islands Trip

6.30am - Gatwick Airport

At last, something exciting is happening. I am off on my Gourmet Break/ Business trip to the Channel Islands. Today I am flying to Guernsey where I have appointments with three shops. Tomorrow I fly to Alderney for two appointments and then back to Guernsey. The next day is Jersey and then home. I check my suitcase into the hold - it contains nothing but samples of various candles, reed diffusers and a new range of bath products. Due to this, my clothes etc have to go in my carryon luggage which I am now wheeling through Security feeling like a Jet Setter.

7.00am - Shopping

I do love airports. They are so exciting and busy. There are so many people going off to some really cool places. I like to spend at least an hour in the shops air-side, spraying on perfume, buying trashy magazines and stocking up on Haribos for the journey.

7.30am - Walking to the Gate

Typical! The gate has been called and mine is miles

away. I'll have to run along the travelators like Usain Bolt to get there in time. I blame the queue for the magazines and sweets! I always seem to get in a pickle with the self-service checkout and forget to put the item in the bag before scanning the next one. The volume is also so loud on them, announcing to all and sundry any little mistake you make. You always seem to have to wait for ages for an assistant to rectify your mistakes, it is better just to brave the queue in my opinion. As I start running, I hear a beeping noise behind me and turning around I see one of those golf cart things that transport disabled passengers bearing down on me. It screeches to a halt and I see Bill, my Mum's next-door neighbour driving it.

"Maddie, I thought I recognised you, your hair gave it away," he laughed.

"Do you want a lift? Joanie here won't mind, would you love?"

Joanie is sitting on the back with her leg in plaster and smiles happily at me.

"No, the more the merrier."

"Well if you're sure, I could do with the lift as my flight has been called and the gates in Brighton!"

"Hop on then Love and I'll have you there in no time."

This is so cool. I feel very important. Joanie is great fun. She broke her leg at a New Year's Eve party in the New Forest. Apparently, she was Limbo dancing at the time and misjudged it and fell off the decking. She is off to see her sister in France for a few days R&R.

As we fly along scattering people in our wake, I suddenly do a double take. It can't be? I think I see MMM striding along the travellator! I am probably mistaken; it must be someone that looks like him and because I can't stop thinking about him, I think I see him everywhere.

Craning my neck, I try to get another look but obviously, these things are faster than they look and we have passed in a flash. Oh well never mind.

We drop Joanie off at her gate and then it's on to mine. There it is gate 75 - BA1231 to Guernsey. Thanking Bill and slipping him a packet of Haribos I show my ticket and passport and find a seat. Great, time to read my celebrity magazine. Fleetingly I remember that I should really be reading the self-help book - How to be a Sales Superhero - but decided I would rather read about the rich and famous and imagine that I am one of them. After all, "We become what we think about most of the time."

Laughing to myself I crack open the first packet of gummy bears and settle down for an absorbing read, putting my feet up on my wheelie case.

After about 20 minutes I am aware of somebody standing in front of me. Looking up, I am shocked to see MMM, looking every inch the successful business traveller. I was right. It was him! He looks every bit as gorgeous as I remember and flashes me a sexy smile.

"Miss Brown, I thought that I saw you flashing past

me on the way," he says grinning at me.

I grin back and then with horror realise that he has clocked the celebrity magazine and raised his eyes questioningly. Quickly I put my feet down, close the magazine and make a big show of taking, 'How to be a Sales Superhero' out of my bag as though collating the two together and returning them to their positions in my bag.

He arches his eyebrows and a smile tugs at the corners of his mouth.

"Oh, I see you are reading, how to be a Sales Superhero, it's a good book, very informative, some may even say, exciting."

"Oh that, yes I have read it many times, I like to call it, my Bible as I really can't live without it." Once again, he raises his eyes in an amused fashion and luckily, we are distracted by the call to board. Phew, any minute now and he would have started testing me.

Note to self - Read, how to be a Sales Superhero, as a matter of urgency!

Anyway, why is he here? He walks with me down the tunnel and we take up our positions in the queue to board.

"This is a happy coincidence Mr Sinclair, what takes you to Guernsey?"

"Please call me James. I have a business meeting with Simpsons, which is quite good timing as I may be able to introduce you in person - that is if you

have the time?"
He suddenly looks a little unsure of himself which brings out a more vulnerable side to him which surprises me.
"Well only if it's today because I am going to Alderney tomorrow."
He looks surprised. "Alderney? Who on earth goes there? There can't be that many business opportunities as it is so small."
"When I cover an area James, nothing is too small." Huh, good answer I am proud of myself.
We get to the door of the plane and the stewardess directs me to my seat. I can't wait to text Matty and tell him that MMM is here. As I find my seat, I feel excited that I have run into him again, it's fate it must be.
Good a window seat.
Suddenly he is behind me in the aisle and I say, "Oh sorry, do you want to get past."
"Actually, that is my seat," he says pointing to the one next to me.
What!! How that can be possible?
"How funny," I say - why did I say that, what does that even mean? It's not funny at all - coincidence, strange, unexpected, but not funny!
I feel a bit flustered now and think that I must have turned bright red. Avoiding eye contact I say, "I won't be long, I'll just stow my bag and coat."
James looks at me with a smile and says, "Allow me," and taking my bag he effortlessly places it in the overhead compartment. As I undo my coat, he

looks at me with an amused expression, oh yes, I remember the last time I took my coat off in front of him I was missing an item of clothing.
Lowering my eyes, I pass him my coat revealing a smart navy-blue shift dress with matching jacket and killer jewellery. He smiles at me, although he does look disappointed at the lack of a floor show. Squashing into the seat I am suddenly aware of how intimate a plane can be. As he sits down next to me his leg brushes against mine and a charge of electricity shoots through me - it's either the effect he has on me or polyester on polyester. A whole hour of conversation with MMM, what if he tests me on his speech? What if he wants to discuss, "How to be a Sales Superhero?"
I start fidgeting which I always do when I am nervous. Luckily the plane starts taxiing out and the sound of engines coupled with the safety demonstration drowns out any would be conversation.
I love taking off on a plane. I always get a pure adrenalin rush as it hurtles down the runway at top speed. As it lifts off, it is all I can do to stop myself raising my arms in the air and shouting Whoa!!
James is looking at me with an amused expression. "You like flying then?"
Is it that obvious? "Yes, I love it especially taking off and landing. In fact, I like all sorts of fairground rides as well."
He laughs, "I'm with you on that, it's a shame there's no time to find a fairground in Guernsey."

Goodness, I wish!
"So, Miss Brown."
"Oh, call me Maddie, everyone does."
"Ok Maddie, how did your meeting go the other night?"
He is looking at me really intently and for a minute I don't know what he is talking about. Then it dawns on me, Trolley man meeting, gosh why is he even interested?
"Oh yes, it went well. Turns out Rob is a Fireman and had some really cool stories to tell."
He suddenly looks disappointed; maybe he was hoping he was the Supermarket Slayer.
"He came around a few days ago and installed smoke alarms for us."
James looks aghast. "You didn't invite a stranger back to your flat, did you?"
"Well yes actually, but it was alright my neighbour Darren was there, and we all got Chinese." James looks even more displeased. "So, tell me about your neighbour," he says looking disconcerted.
"Well, we call him Cardigan Darren, given his love of cardigans. He works in the local supermarket and buys us our food in the past their sell-by date staff shop."
James looks aghast; I am enjoying myself. "He has a bit of a crush on me but I would never go there, he is more like an annoying brother to me. Anyway, we had a great night while he told us about his plans to become a masseuse - don't ask, it's a long story."
"So, getting back to the Fireman, do you have any

more meetings arranged?"
He is looking at me really earnestly and I suddenly realise that he is a little too interested in this subject for normal conversation, is he jealous? No don't be silly, why on earth would he be jealous of him.
"I've left it that I'll ring him when I get back from my trip to arrange another one."
"And will you?" he looks despondently at me.
"I haven't decided yet, he is nice but I am not sure that there is any chemistry there."
Is that relief on his face? No, his face is once again the self-assured business magnate that I know and love.
LOVE!! Don't be so ridiculous, you haven't met him long enough to, Love, anything about him. Anyway, this conversation is way too personal for my liking.
He carries on. "So, who is the 'we' that you refer to in your flat?"
Once again, he is looking anxiously at me.
Goodness, I feel like I am being interrogated. "Oh, my flatmate and best friend Ginge."
He is looking even more confused and I stifle a giggle. "She's an Air Stewardess, and we met at school and have been besties ever since."
He looks relieved. We are interrupted by the drinks trolley coming past and I notice the stewardess giving James a very appreciative look. She is so obviously flirting with him but he seems oblivious to it.
"Water please," he says smiling at her. God that

smile is gorgeous! I really want a coke but he probably thinks that coke should be illegal or something, flashback to his talk about how you should minimise your sugar intake to stay alert and healthy. The Haribos were probably classed as Devil food in his book.

"Same," I say disappointed. Water is so boring, why do you think that people invented cordials? At least she throws us some mini pretzels, so all is not lost. When the trolley departs, I decide to direct the conversation away from me and my dysfunctional life. "So, James, where do you live?" and with whom I wonder.

"Oh, I have a flat in London near to my offices. I live alone as I don't have any bestie to share with." He looks amused but I feel sorry for him, what a lonely way to live.

"I am afraid that my work keeps me very busy so my home is just somewhere to sleep."

"Don't you do anything on your days off?"

"I don't really have many days off but when I do, I go to my house in Dorset."

"Really whereabouts? I love Dorset."

"Poole, I have a boat there too and it helps me blow the cobwebs of London away. I wish I could get there more often but work always comes first."

I sit silently digesting what he has told me.

Suddenly being a mega-rich businessman doesn't seem that appealing, I mean what is the point if you don't have friends or people to share it with. God, this water is so boring and I could murder a Haribo.

The thought of them in the overhead locker is almost too much to bear.
"So where are you staying when you get there?" he suddenly asks.
"Oh, Harbour Spa and Retreat," I say suddenly remembering with excitement the Gourmet Break that I have lined up.
Looking surprised he says. "Scentastic must be doing very well to provide you with 5* accommodation."
I blush and reply. "Actually, I booked a special deal, it's a Gourmet Break which has cost the company only a fraction more than my usual B&B as it includes car hire and meals, plus I get a complimentary massage and a taster menu at Michele's, with wine thrown in. Please don't tell Betty though, sorry Elizabeth, I don't want to give her any more ammunition against me at our 1-1"
He looks stunned and slowly a huge smile breaks out across his face and his eyes crinkle up at the corners, as I noticed at the sales meeting. He starts laughing and I join in.
What a great time we are having, shame we're nearly there, really.
"Maddie, you make me laugh. I don't think that I have ever met anyone like you before."
He carries on laughing - I always have this effect on people.
The seatbelt sign clicks on and we are beginning our descent into Guernsey. Yippee! Landing adrenalin rush imminent.

Guernsey Airport 9.30am

Waiting for our luggage at Baggage re-claim it strikes me that I don't even know how long James is here for and where he is staying. "James, where are you staying?"
He looks at me and raises his eyebrow a smile dancing across his lips. "Well it's funny, but I am staying at The Harbour Spa and Retreat."
I know he is just using my word, but actually when you think about it is kind of funny.
"Do you need a lift there? I am picking up a hire car and would be happy to drive you." I say looking at him hoping that he will say yes. For some reason, I want to prolong our encounter for as long as possible.
"Well I was going to get a cab, but how could I refuse such a generous offer?"

Avis Car Hire Desk 9.45am

The receptionist looks at me and pushes the necessary paperwork over the desk for me to sign.
"I just need your signature here and here," she says indicating where I am to sign with a big cross next to the signature line.
Why don't they just print a cross on these forms? everybody does it these days, from the Doctors to the hotel.
"If you could just enter your pin into the machine,

then that will be the extra insurance covered." Ok, trouble is my mind has just gone blank. What is my pin number? Usually, I have the same one for all of my cards but this one is new and I haven't got around to changing it yet. Panic stations!

MMM is looking at me, probably wondering why I am hesitating. I start to feel hot and bothered. What will I do? The queue behind me sensing trouble start to fidget.

Then with a big sigh of relief, I remember that Ginge had said that this was bound to happen when I received it. She wrote the pin number on the bottom of my right foot with a permanent marker pen for emergencies.

Gosh, she knows me better than I know myself sometimes. The trouble is I need to take off these boots and socks and try to look at the bottom of my feet while maintaining a ladylike pose, all in front of the smiling receptionist and MMM.

"I'm sorry about this, it's a new card. I just need to retrieve the pin number and then we can get off. James, would you mind just helping me out?"

I smile at him and he looks back at me with a puzzled expression. Quickly I start removing my right boot and then the sock. Both of them look at each other not quite sure what is going on. The queue behind have all stopped chatting and are looking at the floor show.

Lifting my foot up I say, "Sorry James, please can you read this out and I will punch it in."

James looks at my foot as I wobble precariously on

one leg, holding onto the counter at the same time. He obviously finds this amusing as his eyes crinkle again and his mouth twitches. He reads out the number quietly and I punch it in. The sooner I change this the better, now the pin is out of the bag, or in this case boot.

Trying to look like this is a normal event I thank him and put my sock and boot back on. The receptionist smiles at me - I bet she has never had this happen before. She gives me the keys and directs us to where we can pick up the car.

As we move away, the queue starts to clap and laugh. I grin at them and make a dignified exit, with James bringing up the rear, wheeling both of our cases behind him.

10.30 Harbour Spa and Retreat.
Just checked in. Wow, this place is amazing. James has gone to his room, and I have found mine. I can see the sea and there is apparently an award-winning garden to explore.

The trouble is I have to just leave my bags as I have three appointments to go to first.

5.30pm Harbour Spa and Retreat.
Finally, I can relax. It is difficult negotiating around an unfamiliar Island with no Sat Nav.

The customers were great, I always love my Guernsey customers, and the scenery is beautiful. Right, time to order my complimentary tea/coffee from room service. For some reason, they don't

provide you with kettles in your room.
As I look outside, I think that I may explore the award-winning garden after my tea, I should have time before dinner. However, first I can't resist texting Matty.

Text to Matty

Hi Matty
You will never guess what's happened.
I'm in Guernsey and MMM's here!

Text from Matty

Tosser?

Text to Matty

Yes MMM

Text from Matty

Has he motivated you yet?

Text from Maddie

Oh yes!

Text from Matty

Be careful, not sure I trust

a man in Ralph Lauren

Text to Matty

Really? You're so ridiculous sometimes. What's wrong with Ralph Lauren?

Text from Matty

Says flash to me.

Text to Matty

You're probably right. Got to go room service knocking

Text from Matty

Enjoy!

I open the door and a waiter delivers my complimentary tea and coffee, well tea actually, on a silver tray with a plate of biscuits. Heaven! Should I tip him? Well, it is meant to be complimentary and I wouldn't give a tip if there was a kettle in my room. Guilt overtakes me and I give him £1- better than nothing.
As soon as the waiter leaves my phone buzzes.

Text from James Sinclair

Hi Maddie
I hope that you had a good day.
I am meeting Mr Simpson for dinner in the hotel. Would you care to join us? I have booked a table for 7.30pm.
James

Text to James Sinclair

Thank you I had a good day. I would love to, shall I meet you in reception at 7.20pm?

Text from James Sinclair

Perfect. Look forward to it.

So, all is going well. I drink my tea while looking out over the Bay. A whole evening with James. I feel excited. I know that it is a business dinner but I still can't wait to see him again.

6.30pm

I decide to take a stroll around the award-winning gardens. However, I am quite disappointed. The standard can't be that high over here because my Mum's garden is better. I mean really, there aren't many flowers and I am sure that half of the plants here are weeds.

There is an odd bench dotted around and is that a statue of an Anchor? How predictable. If I had a statue, it would be much more thought-provoking than an Anchor. I think one of a girl standing there in Bronze with her dress billowing in the breeze, holding her hand up to her eyes as though searching for her lost love, who never returned from his expedition around the world, would be much better. He has been feared drowned, but every day she returns to this same spot and waits for him, ever hoping and praying for his safe return. I wipe a tear from my eye, that is so beautiful and thought-provoking.

Note to self: Leave idea in the room, written on hotel complimentary pad.

7.20pm - Business Dinner

James is waiting for me as I get to the reception. He looks gorgeous and my heart flips when he looks at me. "Maddie, you look great. Come and meet Roger Simpson, the owner of Simpson's" I look at the man standing next to James and see a fairly old man of about 60 years old with thinning hair and a very distinctive paunch. He is smiling at me and I warm to him instantly. He holds out his hand to me which I shake firmly.

"I am very pleased to meet you Maddie; James has

told me so much about you already."
His eyes slide over to James and then back to me and then he winks at me!
What does that mean? Does he have a nervous twitch? Oh, I hope not because if he does it will totally ruin my evening. I will be looking out for it all the time and won't be able to concentrate. James interrupts, "Shall we go through to the restaurant now?"
We follow him and in no time at all, I decide that I like Roger. He seems really pleasant, not at all what I expected. I don't know what I did expect, but it wasn't to warm to someone instantly like this.
After we order I listen to them talking business. It appears that Roger wants James to run a campaign to advertise his stores not just in the Channel Islands but also on the mainland as he is thinking of opening a new store in Southampton. Now I have been to his stores over here and they are hardly cutting edge. The average age of his customers must be 50 years old and they cater for them only. I wouldn't buy much in them as they are quite old fashioned and dated. It's ok over in the Channel Islands because they are firmly established and are the only department store, but even I know that their business model wouldn't work in Southampton. Once they have finished discussing the campaign, Roger looks across at me and says. "So, Maddie, James tells me that you sell a range of scented products. Apparently, we don't currently stock them. Why do you think that is?"

I look at James and he smiles at me reassuringly.
"Well Roger before I answer that can I ask you a question?"
He looks surprised and so does James. "Well of course my dear."
"How long has you buyer worked for you? Miss Baxter is the contact name that I have."
"Oh Jenny, well she must have been with me for about thirty years. She is one of my most loyal staff members."
"I thought so; ok I can answer your question now. The fact is we are not given an appointment to showcase our product because Jenny doesn't need us to."
He looks surprised and confused and so does James. I continue.
"Your buyer has probably dealt with the same rep for about 20 years. I know the ranges that you stock and the agent has been with that particular company for that length of time. Over the years, they would have built up a good working relationship and a real friendship. They trust each other and all the time the company is bringing out new ranges, and the product is selling, there is no reason to change. You may grow by 5-10% each year which keeps everyone happy. In these circumstances, you find that things only change when one of them leaves. That is why the large department stores tend to move their buyers around every 2 years or so. That way they don't form strong bonds with their reps and fresh ideas come in as people have different

perceptions on how things work. They also constantly change and update their ranges to reflect the current trends, therefore moving with the times and keeping their customers interested."

Both men are looking at me, obviously stunned. I carry on. "So, you see Roger, the only time that I, or anyone else, will get to showcase our products, is when something changes within the buying department of your stores."

Roger looks thoughtfully at James who stares back at him with a faint smile.

Roger replies, "So you are saying that we are old fashioned."

Gosh, I hope that I haven't offended him.

I reply. "To a degree yes. You are protecting your customer base, not wanting to alienate your regular customers. However, the trick is to get your customers to move with you, as well as attracting new ones. There are many ways that you can do this and I would probably advise you to look around the various shops in Southampton and on the mainland before you open your new store. You can take a lot from this and possibly use your new store opening to try a different approach."

I know that I have come on strong but I really do have nothing to lose. Jenny won't ever agree to see me, anyway.

Roger looks thoughtful, and we are interrupted by the starter arriving. I am starving and attack the smoked salmon parcel with delight. James smiles at me and looks, dare I say, impressed with my little speech. For some reason, his approval gives me a glow inside. I want to impress him. I smile back at him enjoying the evening.

The conversation turns to more general things and we hear about Roger's family and how he started the store all those years ago. I tell them about my experiences, although I leave most of the more exciting ones out, I am in a business meeting after all.

The tea and coffee arrives and Roger says, "Well Maddie, you have given me much to think about. I understand that you are in Jersey on Friday. I too will be there and if you have the time, I would very much like to meet up at the store to show you around and perhaps discuss any business opportunities that I may pass your way."

Trying to look composed and nonchalant I reply, "That would be great Roger, what time suits you?"

"Shall we say 12 pm? I could buy you lunch afterwards, if you have time."

Wow, in your face Betty and Jenny for that matter. It is all agreed and Roger says his goodbyes leaving me with James - Did Roger just wink at me again?!

"So, Maddie, you surprise me once again."

James says looking at me with his gorgeous smile playing around his lips.

"Obviously, you are a Sales Superhero, judging by that performance."

I smile back at him triumphantly; people always underestimate me. I quite like it really because then they are surprised by what I have to say.

"Well I believe that -it's not what you know but who you know- as I think I have just proved."
"Well, I wouldn't argue with you there, but that only gets you so far. It's what you do afterwards that counts. Anyway, if it's not too late would you like to get a drink at the bar?"
I nod and we make our way out to the bar.
I order a white wine spritzer and we find a seat nearby. After some more obvious flirting and banter and not just from me, James suddenly looks serious and alarm fills me.
"Maddie, I have to leave in the morning but I have really enjoyed your company."
"Me too," I say smiling at him
"I was just wondering if when you get back, we could arrange our own meeting, say over dinner, but only if you want to?" he says looking suddenly unsure of himself.
"I would like that," I say suddenly feeling really happy inside, maybe it's the wine but I doubt it.
A smile breaks out over his face and it really lights up, is that relief I see? No, I am sure that he goes for "meetings" all the time and has probably never been turned down.

He walks me to my room, I feel a bit awkward, should I invite him in for a complimentary tea or coffee? However, he just says, "Thank you for a lovely evening, I have really enjoyed it. Please take care on the rest of your trip and I will look forward to our meeting when you get back. Oh and good

luck at Simpson's, he really liked you, I could tell."
"Thank you, James, I really do appreciate your help. It was most kind of you to put yourself out for me. Have a good trip home."
We both stand here, just smiling awkwardly at each other. James looks as though he is about to say something else but then appears to think better of it; instead he just smiles and heads off towards his room.

January 13th Guernsey Airport 9.30am

I am heading out to the tarmac to board my flight to Alderney. The plane that is taking us there is only a little plane that holds 12 people.
We have to wait by the wing to be called as you have to sit 2x2 and all get in a different door. I am annoyingly last to be called and as I get in, I notice several pairs of male eyes turning to look at me. How did I not notice that I was the only female on this flight?
"Welcome to our Stag weekend," one of the lads say with a grin.
What!!! I smile at them all but have to ask. "Of all places to go why are you going to Alderney? Surely there's not a lot there to cater for a Stag weekend."
"Yes, we are asking ourselves the same question," quipped one cheeky looking chap.
I soon learned that the guy behind me was the Groom so I looked around and say, "Oh congratulations by the way."
The chap next to me laughed and said cheekily, "You haven't seen his wife to be."
"Is she your sister then?" I retort to howls of laughter. Goodness call himself a friend, I hope that he's not the Best man.
Once the plane sets off, there is no conversation, as anybody knows that has journeyed in a light

aircraft. The noise of the engines is deafening. Ear plugs are advisable but none were offered.

It is a windy day, and the flight is proving very bumpy. Not a bad way to go to heaven with a planeload of hunky men!

As we touch down, I notice that we appear to have missed the runway altogether. It is now adjacent to us and we have landed on a strip of grass instead. Has this Pilot even got a licence? I very much doubt it!

As we taxi in, the hailstones start battering the plane; this is not a good omen for my trip! We disembark and race for the terminal, or in this case the shed calling itself the terminal.

Finally, I make it out of arrivals. Looking around, I notice my customer who has kindly offered to pick me up from the Airport. She directs me to her VW Beetle and I heave my heavy case into the Boot.

"That was an interesting plane load." she states looking at me and grinning.

"Yes, apparently a Stag weekend," I say laughing.

She raises her eyebrows, "I can't think why they have come here, it's hardly Ibiza."

"Maybe they're into country pursuits rather than the other kind," I say wryly.

Jeanette, my customer owns the largest shop on the Island, a sort of general store where she sells most things. They get through quite a lot of candles here due to the number of power cuts, so she is actually quite a good account.

She takes me to the only Hotel on the Island for

coffee and to do the order. Once we have taken care of business, she kindly takes me on a tour of the Island. Afterwards, she drops me off to my next appointment. "Call me when you're finished and I'll take you to the Airport," she says generously.

Now anybody who has been to Alderney knows that the High street consists of very few shops. The cobbled streets don't appear to like my wheelie case, and it is hard work. As I stagger up to the shop, I notice with alarm that it has a sign on the door - 'Closed for Lunch 1 pm - 2.30pm' The time is now 1.50pm. What on earth am I going to do for 40 minutes here? There is nothing else open and I can't go far because of the heavy suitcase. For goodness' sake, who closes for lunch these days? The Tourist Information shop is next door - also closed for lunch! - and I study every last bit of information in the window while praying that it doesn't hail again.

Then I sit on my suitcase outside the darkened shop window thinking murderous thoughts. I mean for goodness' sake, I have travelled hundreds of miles, endured a near plane crash and my customer couldn't have lunch another time! When we made the appointment, it was for 2 pm, she must have known she would be closed then!

I am suddenly aware of a lady running up the street waving and shouting, "I'm here! I'm sorry I am late."

"No problem," I say smiling sweetly, which is the complete opposite of how I am feeling. I do want her to order after all.

7.30pm - Michele's Michelin Star Restaurant - Guernsey

Well, I made it back with no dramas just in time for my complimentary neck and shoulder massage in the Spa and now I am walking up to the renowned Michele's Michelin Star restaurant for my Gourmet meal for one. I find myself in front of two great doors and on entering am thrown into the world of the elite of dining.
A waiter comes up and says, "Are you here for Sex in the City?" What sort of place is this?
"Oh, no just a meal," I reply thinking how progressive these Restaurants are these days.
Looking around, I realise that there is a group of very posh ladies dressed in designer outfits and headgear - they look like Fascinators. Whoever invented those? Probably some hat designer who had run out of material. It appears that they are on a "Sex in The City" themed evening. There is lots of raucous laughter and they appear to be having a great time.
I am taken through the throng of excited women to my solitary table for one. My thoughts turn to James and I wish that he was here with me.
The table is set to overlook the Bay with my back to the rest of the restaurant. The lights are dim and there is no candle on the table. I can't even read my

book it is so dark; all I can do is stare straight ahead. My waiter asks if I would like a glass of wine, so I order a Shiraz- my favourite. I'm bored with my own company already, I know, I'll get my iPad out and read that new book I downloaded. It has night vision, so I am sorted.

Now where is it, oh yes here it is, "How to be a millionaire through Sales."

The restaurant starts to fill up and there is still no sign of my first course. Goodness me the service is appalling; I should be on dessert now. Putting the iPad down I look around and the waiter miraculously appears looking worried.

"Sorry to disturb you madam but please can we start the service?" What? Really! They thought I was busy reading! He tells me what they are going to serve as the first course and I am sorry but I have to reject it. Sweetbreads on a salad are not for me. I have nothing against salad but I have seen Master Chef and know exactly what a sweetbread is and delicious or not I am not going to try one. This is meant to be enjoyable not a Bush Tucker Trial. Instead, they give me Calf Livers Pate with a redcurrant sausage. The sausage was delicious but the Calf's Liver was not! What I didn't realise was that with each of the seven courses comes a different wine. The waiter pops up and pours samples into a large wine glass while explaining its qualities. I try to look knowledgeable and nod approvingly. It's not so bad as it is useful to help get the Calf's Liver Pate down.

Another age later the second course arrives. I can only describe it as, Fish Jelly, swimming in fishy water in all its gelatinous glory. Up pops the wine waiter again with a white wine this time, which I normally only like with lemonade. Oh, will this evening never end? I am annoyed because I have just missed the episode of "The Restaurant" that I wanted to see. Now it will bug me as I won't know whose restaurant was closed this week -I wish it was Michele's, I think venomously.

The third course is Duck, with a sort of hash brown type potato on red cabbage and oh yes, another wine to accompany it. By now, Sex in the City has gone and there is tumbleweed blowing around the restaurant. The delay in courses means that all I can do is drink more wine. I really need the toilet but I can't go and risk delaying the proceedings even more. I notice my reflection in the window and see a dejected beaten figure that is being well and truly punished for booking a Gourmet Break on the company. Another course appears which I can only describe as onion ice cream. Truly disgusting. Who in the world ever thought that onion ice cream would be a good thing to make? Not even the accompanying wine can make me down this. I just stare at it in front of me, mocking me on its little plastic holder. Ok, I can do this, I will get to dessert. But no, bearing down on me now is a great table laden with every cheese imaginable accompanied by the port bottle. Enough!! I scream inside, JUST BRING ME THE CHOCOLATE!

Politely I declined the cheese course. At Last! The dessert has arrived, an extremely dark chocolate sorbet, (I hate dark chocolate!) with a vanilla fondant that actually tastes delicious, it's more like a cake than a fondant, oh and yes, it is accompanied by a dessert wine.

Ok, enough is now well and truly enough! I stagger to my feet desperate for the loo - will I even be able to walk? In a not so steady, slightly hysterical voice I ask for the Bill. I can just about make out that I have to add a tip, oh for goodness' sake this trip is now costing a fortune! Will I make it back to my room without falling over? Will I wet myself on the way? Will a knife-wielding Chef accost me in revenge for leaving most of his Gourmet meal?

I stagger back through the award-winning gardens and just make it to my room in time for the wine to finally be freed from my body. My head is spinning with the effects of the alcohol and I am not sure if I will make it through the night. I can't even manage to summon the complimentary tea and coffee I feel so ill.

I will never ever book a Gourmet Break again, I resolve as my head spins me into sleep.

January 14th -8.30am - Reception, Harbour Spa and Retreat

Finally, I am checking out to hop on a plane to Jersey for phase 3 of my mission.

I am a bit worried in case, Gourmet Break is emblazoned in neon ink on my bill. What will Betty say? Maybe I can persuade them to change it to, "Bargain, cheaper than anything else on the Island, Break."

However, in a flash of inspiration and forward planning, I have pinched some headed notepaper from the room and if necessary, will type up my own receipt on my home computer. Forward planning is the key - How to be a Sales Superhero, chapter seven!

5.30pm - BA flight 1232 to Gatwick

Finally, I am on my way home. I don't know how Ginge does it, I am exhausted.

My meeting at Simpson's went very well. Roger met me and gave me a tour of the store. He told me that he had thought long and hard about what I said and had decided that he was going to employ a Retail Consultant to assist him with his new venture and then roll it out to his other stores. He was also going to shake up the buying department and for now, he wanted to order our complete range for both stores to run alongside his existing range as a trial, to monitor the differences in sales. Take that Betty and Jenny!! My other appointments also went well so all in all it was a successful trip.

Now I am looking forward to getting home for a nice long hot bubble bath, a takeaway Pizza, no wine! and hopefully, a box set with Ginge. It seems ages since I last saw her and I have missed her. I can't wait to tell her about James Sinclair. The thought of him makes me smile. When should I text him re our meeting? Maybe baggage reclaim is a bit too eager, I should wait until I get home perhaps?

7.30pm

I am so glad to be home! Trips away appear to drain the life out of me. I thought that Ginge would be back but sadly she has gone away again; I always seem to miss her these days. This time she is in Los Angeles. Tommy lives there and the band are on a break from the tour. She has taken a week off to spend it with him. I can't wait to hear the gossip when she gets back. I will have some of my own to tell her after this Channel Islands trip. Speaking of which, despite my jet lag I must text Mmm. I just can't wait to set up this meeting as I haven't thought of anything else since he suggested it. However, before I could even grab my phone it pinged into life.

Text from James Sinclair

Hi Maddie
I hope you had a good trip and the Simpsons meeting went ok.
Are you free for our meeting on Saturday. I could pick you up at 7 pm if you text me your address?
Hopefully Yours
James

HOPEFULLY YOURS!

Text to James Sinclair

Hi James
The trip was great and Simpsons deal done and dusted thanks to you. I am free on Saturday at 7 pm address 15 Parkmead, Esher.
Looking forward to it,
Maddie x

Oh no, I've pressed send and I've put a kiss on it! The trouble is I always do this and forget when I'm texting who is a friend and who is business. I am sure that it doesn't hurt business, it just makes me seem more friendly and approachable, however, when texting Betty there are definitely no kisses. I do like those new emoji's that you can get now. I like to send them instead of a text sometimes. The record to Matty one day was 50 back and forth; it was a competition as to who could send the funniest one. The trouble was it became boring after the first 20 and then neither of us would give up. We learned our lesson and never did it again - you can have too much of a good thing you know.

January 17th 6.50pm

Oh, my God! It's nearly 7 pm and James will be here in a minute and I am having a total wardrobe crisis! He hasn't said what we are doing and I don't know what to wear. Is it a meal? If so, what kind and do I need to dress up? Is it the Cinema? Our local one is freezing. It's ok when you are watching films like The Titanic which help create the mood but a nightmare every other time.

I throw my clothes around the room in a total panic. The doorbell rings and now I am at Defcon 3/ code Red! Grabbing my dressing gown, I hurry to the door.

As I open it, I do a double take and my heart does a strange somersault. James is standing there looking even more gorgeous than I remember wearing smart jeans, a black polo neck jumper and a black leather jacket. He has Timberland boots on and is staring at me once again with an amused expression on his face.

"Hi Maddie, you are looking - late."

I flush remembering my dressing gown.

"I'm so sorry James, please come in I won't be a minute, I promise."

Just then Cardigan Darren pops his head out of his front door like a Rottweiler protecting the premises. The trouble is he is more like a Yorkshire terrier such is the threat that he imposes to a would-be attacker. His eyes narrow as he takes in the scene and says,

"You ok Maddie, is this man trying to sell you something?"

James looks amused and I blush even more. "It's ok Darren, thanks for your concern but James is a friend of mine."

He narrows his eyes again and stares at James. "Ok, but knock on the wall if you need me, I'll be there in an instant."

I bundle James in quickly and we both crease up laughing, but quiet laughter in case Darren can hear us through the wall. Have you ever tried laughing quietly? It's quite strange, really. Once we have stopped laughing, I say, "James take a seat and I'll be about 5 minutes, put the TV on if you want to."

I rush into my room and close the door. Ok jeans, jumper and a short fur jacket with leather ankle boots.

7.05pm

James is sitting casually on the settee flicking through a magazine. Oh no, not the celebrity one again. I rush over and roll my eyes saying, "Oh I'm sorry James; Ginge is forever reading these trashy mags. I am sure there is a Reader's Digest here somewhere."

He laughs at me saying, "There is nothing wrong with a bit of celebrity gossip. It is the weekend after all."

I grin at him liking him more and more and it's only been about 10 minutes.

I lock up and follow him to the parking bays outside. WOW, he has a really cool two-seater BMW, all black and shiny. He opens the passenger door and I almost fall inside. I never did get to finishing school and learn the art of getting in and out of sports cars. They are so low. It's almost as though you are sitting on the road.

James gets in with no such trouble of course. He turns and looks at me and says with a grin, "Well, I hope that you're up for an adrenalin filled evening?"

What on earth does that mean? I look at him questioningly and he carries on.

"Well, as we couldn't get to the fairground in Guernsey, I thought that one in London would have to do. Just remember to scream if you want to go faster."

I am so excited. What a great idea. I laugh and say, "James that's brilliant. I warn you though I am a fairground ride Ninja. You may not be able to keep up."

He starts the engine, "Don't worry, I'll try my best." and then we are off.

9.00pm

We have just had the most fun I can ever remember having on a cold January night. There was not a ride that we didn't go on, even the little merry-go-round rides. We ate hot dogs and tried our hands at all the little games stalls. My favourite was the Big Wheel. It was like being in the North Pole for temperature which gave me the excuse to snuggle up to James in our little seat for two, suspended over London looking at the twinkling lights of the city. He even put his arm around me and I couldn't have been happier.

The Ghost train was also a good excuse to cling on to him, not that I was scared but I am a very good actress when I want to be. This date was pure Genius, by the end of it we were the best of friends and any awkwardness evaporated like the Candy Floss that we ate big bags of.

"Maddie, would you like to get a drink somewhere and warm up?" James offers to which I nod enthusiastically.

As we walk down the cobbled streets of the South Bank, James once again puts his arm around my shoulders.

"I am having a great time Maddie, but then I knew I would from the moment I met you. You make me laugh and I can't remember the last time that I had so much fun."

Suddenly he stops and pulls me around to face him.

"You know I would really like to do this again soon, not the fairground of course but perhaps dinner somewhere, where I can get to know you better."

"I would like that James; I really enjoy your company too." Suddenly I feel quite shy. I realise that I do like him more and more every time I see him and the thought of doing it again fills me with such joy that I can hardly breathe. His eyes crease up again at the corners and I am mesmerised by him and can't look away. He moves closer to me so that our faces are just centimetres apart. I shiver, not just with the cold, for I don't even register the temperature, all I can think about is that I want to kiss him right now.

He leans in and kisses me a soft tender kiss that sends my senses into overdrive. He doesn't stop and we are standing there by the Thames lost in a world of our own, oblivious to the crowds of people passing us by.

He draws away and just looks at me, with such an intense look of happiness and longing, all rolled into one. I smile at him and then boldly touch his face and reach up to kiss him once more. He pulls me closer and once again we are lost in each other.

9.30pm - Milo's Bar and Café, South Bank We are sitting here in a nice warm bar drinking steaming mugs of hot chocolate and cuddling like teenagers. "I don't want tonight to end," James says and I nod agreeing. He carries on. "When I saw you balancing on that chair my first instinct was to save you from falling. When I held you in my arms and you looked at me, I was blown away. Something inside me was triggered and from that moment on, all I could think about was you. When I found out that you had a date, I was desperate, I could think of nothing else that evening and was praying that nothing would come of it. When you texted and said that it was progressing well, I was eaten up with jealousy that I have never felt before."

I look at him surprised. "I never realised any of this James. The thing is as soon as I met you, Trolley Man was history. He never really stood a chance. I couldn't believe it when fate put us on that flight to Guernsey. It was as if it was meant to be."

James suddenly looks sheepish. "Oh, yes, well I am afraid I have a confession to make about that."

He is looking at me anxiously and suddenly I realise that fate must have had no hand in that at all. He carries on. "I rang your company to find out when your trip was planned and asked which hotel you were using, as I wanted to arrange a meeting with Simpsons. They told me and so I booked the same flight and hotel."

My face must look a picture because he suddenly looks very worried. "I hope that you don't think I'm a mad stalker, but it was the only way that I could think of to see you again. I saw you check in and asked the check-in agent to put me next to you as we were friends."

I look at him in astonishment. Nobody has ever gone to such extreme lengths to be with me in my life. How on earth could I be annoyed?

Suddenly the humour of the situation engulfs me and I burst out laughing. The relief on his face is apparent as he joins in.

"Ok James Sinclair, your plan has worked out spectacularly well. I am extremely flattered and touched that you have gone to so much trouble. Now, what can I do to reward your tenacity." Once again, I lean towards him and kiss him gently on the lips.

10.30pm

As we walk towards the car, James stops by the embankment and leans on the rail looking out over the Thames. He is holding my hand now, and it all seems so right and natural. He looks at me and I can see via the lamplight that his expression is suddenly unsure again. "Maddie, I hope you don't think I am trying anything on here, but I would really like to spend tomorrow with you as well. I'm a workaholic and usually don't have days off and know that come Monday morning, work will take over again."

Looking at him I smile happily. "I would love that James, what do you have in mind?"

"Well, my flat is very near to here, just around this corner actually and I was wondering if you would like to stay tonight, in the spare room of course. Then we could spend the day together tomorrow. Please say no if you feel uncomfortable and I will drive you straight home and pick you up again in the morning."

Oh, this is unexpected. My first instinct is to say, YES, but what if it makes me look bad? I mean, there is a name for a girl who stays the night with someone on a first date and that is most definitely not me. On the other hand, he does have a spare room, but what if he turns out to be a psycho? I could end up on the news and they would say, "If only she hadn't gone back to his flat silly girl." I do want to though and something tells me that I would be perfectly safe with him. He is looking at me anxiously, so I say, "Well it is a bit irregular, but there is no harm in me coming back for a coffee and then maybe, we'll have to see."

He smiles at me and I really can't resist it. He has such an open and honest face, nothing at all like the e-fits you see on Crime watch.

"Come on then it is getting really chilly now and I don't want to be responsible for you catching a cold on our first date."

A date is it now? It started out as a meeting. This is the first time that a meeting has turned into a date, but then I have never been to a meeting like it before either.

10.45pm - Thames View Apartments

James wasn't kidding when he said he only lives around the corner. His flat is in a block of really swanky apartments overlooking the Thames. I can even see, The Houses of Parliament. The flat is on the top floor and is on the corner with a balcony running around it. It is like something out of a magazine. The furnishings are tastefully done, very modern and up to date, oh what's that expression? Bang on trend. I do know what I am talking about as I am an avid fan of 60-minute makeover.

"James, this flat is amazing. You obviously have a talent for Interior design. Have you lived here long?"

"No, about six months. I used to live in Chelsea, but this is nearer my office so I rent that one out now and moved here to be closer. As far as the Interior is concerned, I must hold my hands up and admit that I paid an Interior Designer to do it as I don't have the time."

"Well, she has done a really good job." I note the soft cream furry rug on the floor and picture me and James entwined on it.

Note to self - stop having lustful thoughts towards love interest on the first date. Wait until the second at least.

James takes my jacket. "Would you like coffee? And I'm sure I have a packet of biscuits here somewhere."

Now you're talking my language. I nod and follow him into the kitchen. Wow again! This space is huge, nothing like our little kitchen in Esher. The units are polished wood and the doors have no handles, you just push them and they open. The rest is marble tops and stainless steel and joy upon joy, is that a coffee machine I see built into the unit? I can just see myself as a Barista, conjuring up all types of new and exotic coffee combinations here.

I sit on a high bar stool and watch him in action. Within minutes he has whipped up two Lattes and rustled up a plate of exotic looking biscuits. He must think a lot of me as these are definitely not the builder's biscuits that I usually have. I say builder's biscuits, because I overheard someone in Waitrose once, saying to her husband, that she must get some "ordinary biscuits for the builders." Some people don't live in the real world.

We take our coffees and head out onto the balcony. Where is my Jacket? This man obviously doesn't feel the cold, this date is now getting a bit too outdoorsy for my liking and I am freezing. I cup my hands around the mug for extra warmth and shiver. James looks concerned and flicks a switch on the wall. Suddenly a nearby heater springs into life and throws out some considerable heat. Gosh, my fireman friend would probably think this was illegal or something in a flat.

We sit down on a nearby comfy seat. It has large cream cushions that look brand new and there are various ornamental topiary dotted around.

We sit close together looking at the lights and taking in the sounds of the bustling city that never sleeps. This is heaven, all we can see from our window in Esher is the communal car park. I could stay out here all night; however, I can't help myself and start yawning.

James looks at me and smiles. "Come on Maddie, you look like you need your sleep. If I show you the spare room you can decide if you want to stay here. If you would rather, I could drive you home."

He pulls me up and we go inside. The spare bedroom is amazing. It has patio doors that lead out onto the balcony and what a view! This room is bigger than mine at home and as with the rest of the flat, it is tastefully decorated. The bed looks so cosy and inviting that my mind is instantly made up.

"There is an ensuite here and you can find anything you may need in there. If you want, I can find you one of my t-shirts to sleep in. The door does lock from the inside so you will be perfectly safe."

He is looking at me anxiously and I decide to give in, after all, what harm will it do? The thought of driving back to Esher is not a pleasant one.

"Thanks, James, it's kind of you. I wouldn't mind something to change into though."

He looks pleased and is probably relieved that he doesn't have to drive to Esher at this late hour. Taking my hand, he says, "No problem follow me and you can choose something."

A WALK-IN WARDROBE! James has every girl's dream! It is wall to wall shelving and hanging space and is HUGE!

"I'll leave you to choose something; I have to make a call."

At this time of night! Who on earth could he be calling now?

I have a great time sifting through James's clothes, you can tell a lot about a person by the clothes they wear. He has lots of smart suits and obviously doesn't do much washing as his shirts are still in their dry-cleaning wrappers. His bill must be huge. There are many pairs of jeans and casual tops, with almost a whole unit devoted to boots and shoes.

I resist the urge to rummage through his underwear drawer; some things are just too personal, although I am tempted. I can't see any pyjamas, so finally decide on a long-sleeved t-shirt that covers more than my Tunic did when I first met him. There is a dressing gown on the back of the door so I grab that too.

12.00pm

Bliss! I love this bed. It is so warm and cosy. I can lay here and look out of the window at the Thames. Actually, I think I'll draw the curtains as you never know who may be around with their binoculars.

That's better. James was really sweet and made sure that I had everything. I was a bit surprised that he never kissed me goodnight, but it was probably for the best. It is our first date after all.

I couldn't believe how much stuff he had in the ensuite. Most of it was amenity packs from various airlines stuffed in a drawer, but there was also some Jo Malone bath oil and soap. I never had him down as the type that would buy from that establishment. Maybe it's the influence of a former girlfriend? That's annoying, the thought of another woman here is somehow faintly disturbing.

I wonder what he is doing now?

January 18th - 10am

The sound of voices wakes me and for a minute I forget where I am. Then it all comes flooding back. Oh no, I feel a bit awkward now. James is going to see me with bed hair and no makeup! I quickly jump out of bed and head for the shower.

This shower is fantastic; it has jets that massage you all around. I can use the travel shampoo and conditioner and luckily, I have my make up in my bag.

Once I have showered and cleaned my teeth with the toothbrush in the amenity kit- hmm British Airways, First Class, not bad, I get dressed and do my makeup and am nervous to head outside my room. Oh well here goes nothing.

As I go into the kitchen, I am surprised to see James talking to a man, who is sitting on the bar stool, drinking a cappuccino. James smiles at me and the man looks up with a shocked expression.

"Morning Maddie, I hope you slept well. Come in and I'll make you a coffee. This is Jeremy, my assistant."

Jeremy looks surprised, but still jumps down and offers me his hand.

"I'm pleased to meet you, Maddie. Sorry if I look surprised but you are the first person that I have ever seen here apart from James and Hatty."

HATTY WHO! James sees my face and laughs.

"Hatty is my housekeeper. She comes in three times a week and cleans and does my laundry and shopping. There is probably nothing here that she hasn't bought."

Well she has good taste that's for sure, I think remembering the Jo Malone.

I decide that I like the look of Jeremy, but am surprised as I thought that James would have had a female assistant. Jeremy laughs and says,

"Yes, Hatty is great with a great name. She is called Hatty Tatty; don't you think that's a brilliant name?"

Laughing I agree. I think that I could get along very well with Jeremy.

James however, draws this little gathering to a close.

"Jeremy has just dropped by with some paperwork for me. I had to leave early on Saturday and it needs to be done by the morning. Thanks, Jeremy, enjoy the rest of your day and I'll see you in the morning."

"No problem, nice to meet you, Maddie."

I smile at him as he leaves. Looking at James I say,

"Do you expect your staff to work on Sundays as well, James?"

He laughs,

"Not normally but Jeremy offered as he was passing anyway. He is off to meet his partner who works in the West End."

Wow, I'm Impressed.

"What does he do?"

"He's a producer. They are staging a play at, The Garrick Theatre; he virtually lives there. Mind you, Jeremy virtually lives at the office, so they have to meet up when they can."

"Slave driver!"

James suddenly looks at me and his expression softens.

"I had a really good time last night, Maddie. I hope that you did too?"

"Yes, thank you, James. It was, exciting."

He pulls me towards him and says, "Anyway, good morning gorgeous,"

and he kisses me, a gentle good morning sort of kiss.

I am happier now than I have ever been. What a New Year this is turning into.

12pm

We got some breakfast at a nearby Café, which was really cool with all sorts of different people milling around. James suggested that we take the riverboat to Greenwich - he appears to love the cold! - and we had a look around the Cutty Sark.

Now we are heading out of London in his sports car to a Pub he knows for Sunday Lunch.

"So, what time do you start work in the morning James?"

"I usually get in for 7 am and then leave around 8 pm."

That is a serious work ethic!

"So, what do you do for food?"

"Jeremy usually orders in food, or we have a canteen downstairs that is very good."

"Do all your staff work long hours?"

"No, most work the usual 9-6pm but then they do have a life outside of work; I have to keep reminding myself of that sometimes."

I am silent; I wonder where I would fit into this busy schedule. Maybe I won't. This could be a one-off, a distraction. The thought makes me feel depressed. I don't want this to be once in a while thing, I appear to have fallen quite quickly for this man sitting beside me, but where can it go?

"Well James, I may well have to get a job with you and then we can see each other every day."

Oh no, he has gone quiet and his face has hardened. Maybe this is just a fling.

"I'm sorry Maddie, I know that you don't really

mean it but I have a golden rule that I will never break."

"Which is?"

"I never mix business with pleasure. It is a recipe for disaster."

"Wasn't that how we met though?"

"Exceptional circumstances. We weren't at the pleasure stage yet only the business one. Now that I see how much pleasure I get from being with you, there can be no more business involved. I wouldn't want it to come between us."

It makes sense I suppose. Oh well.

"Well James, I wouldn't want to work with you anyway, you appear quite demanding."

I laugh and he joins in.

The Haywagon - Richmond

I've just realised that my phone has run out of charge. Suddenly I feel lost. It's not as if anyone would call me on a Sunday anyway but I feel cast adrift on a sea of no communication. However did people cope before mobile phones?

Note to self - Buy a portable charger and while you're at it a selfie stick. Not strictly necessary but think of the fun that you could have!

The Haywagon is one of those traditional pubs with lots of beams and horseshoes on the walls. It feels cosy and warm and is buzzing with the conversation of its customers. Lots of people have dogs with them and there aren't many spare tables left. We manage to find one luckily and sit in a booth in the corner. We decide that as its Sunday we will order the Roast Beef. Hurray for the invention of the roast dinner.

James orders some wine for me and a soda water for him as he is driving. It feels really cosy sitting here in front of a roaring fire. The boat trip has put some colour in my cheeks - either that or the wine - and I am feeling very content.

Once we have finished James suggests that we go the cinema to watch a film.

6pm

Never go to watch a film with your new flame when there is sex involved. It was really embarrassing not least because it is now all I can think about with him; in fact, I can't even look at him without blushing. I didn't know where to look and just kept on shovelling in the popcorn. I feel really sick. We are both quiet now, like me he is probably re-living every excruciating scene.

7pm

Sadly, we are in my flat and our whirlwind date is over. He pulls into the visitors parking bay and looks at me with a sombre expression.

"Well, here we are."

I feel strangely subdued; I wonder if there will be a next time?

"Yes, thank you, James, I have had a really good time."

James looks as subdued as me. He suddenly looks at me, once again looking unsure.

"Maddie, can we meet up again soon? Do you have much on this week?"

Thank goodness, another date! I can't help a big smile breaking out across my face as I reply,

"Not much, Ginge is home; in fact, she probably arrived earlier today, but otherwise no, just work."

"Would it be ok if we meet up one evening then, say for dinner?"

I nod happily and he leans towards me pulling my head towards his.

I could stay here all night kissing him. It's almost as if the magic will be broken if this date ends.

"Come on, I'll walk you to your door."

Like a couple of teenagers, we head towards the flat kissing in doorways, in the lift and in the corridor.

7.30pm

As I put the key in the lock, I am surprised that the

door is flung open before I even turn the key.

What on earth? The flat is full of people! Suddenly I see my mother with tears streaming down her face racing towards me.

"Maddie! Oh, thank goodness, we thought that you had been abducted."

WHAT! She grabs hold of me as though she will never let go. I can also see my father looking very worried and Cardigan Darren looking extremely anxious.

Then I see Ginge, she looks absolutely terrible, her face is streaked with tears and she is as white as a sheet.

I look at James, who is as bewildered as I am. I pull away from my mother.

"What do you mean abducted? Why on earth would you think that?"

My mum blows her nose into a tissue and gestures wildly at Darren.

"Darren rang us this morning and said that you never came home. He was worried because apparently, he caught some strange man knocking on your door last night. He said that he looked a bit shifty so decided to ring you when you didn't come home and it just went straight through to voicemail."

"It was out of charge," I say weakly, could this be any more embarrassing?

She looks accusingly at James who looks concerned. He steps forward and says.

"I am sorry for any confusion Mrs Brown, my name is James Sinclair and I can assure you that I am no kidnapper."

Mum looks at him her eyes widening. Her look changes from one of worry and fear to one of sudden happiness.

"You were on a date?" she says hopefully and James smiles broadly at her.

"Yes, we were. Maddie stayed at my house, in the spare room of course, because it got late. We spent today together. If we had known that you were worried, we would, of course, have contacted you."

Mum now looks absolutely delighted and grabs hold of his hand.

"Oh James, what must you think of us, please come in and sit down. Darren, you had better ring the Police and stand them down, Oh and the Coastguard."

WHAT!!! I look at Cardigan Darren in shock who now has the grace to look extremely embarrassed. He won't look at me and says,

"We rang the Police to report you as missing; they said that they would notify their patrols to look out for you. We had to email them your photo. We also called the Coastguard in case."

"In case of what?"

He has now gone bright red and mumbles,

"In case your body was dumped at sea."

I can't take this all in, I mean I only stayed at someone's house for the night, ok out of character and something I certainly don't want to be shouted from the rooftops. I mean, they probably think that I am one of those loose women who jump into bed with the first guy that asks them. What do they call it the next day? Ah yes, The Walk of Shame.

This is possibly, The Marathon of Shame.

"Well Darren, I suppose you had better cancel the search party because as you can see, I am fine."

Is that a siren I can hear outside? We all look at each other as the loud wailing of a siren comes even closer and closer. I look wildly around me and Darren once again turns bright red.

"Is that a Fire Engine? Oh, no please don't say you called the Fire Department? What for, in case my body is boarded up under the floor?"

Just then the door flies open and Rob bursts into the room in full uniform, minus the hose luckily. He sees me and relief floods his face.

"Oh Maddie, thank goodness. Darren texted me to say that you had been abducted. I came as soon as I could."

Ok, this is now getting even weirder. James is looking daggers at Rob as he grabs hold of me in a bear hug. Mum and Dad are looking bewildered and

Ginge has still not moved from the settee, what is the matter with her?

I turn as red as Rob's engine.

"Oh, Hi Rob, I am sorry for the false call out. As you can see, I am fine, my phone ran out of charge and I was staying at a friend's."

Rob looks around and then spies James, his eyes narrow as he looks between us both.

"What, him?" he says incredulously.

"Um yes, James."

Rob looks shocked and who could blame him. I was meant to ring him when I got back from my trip and I hadn't and now here I was with someone else. I feel really bad. He looks around and then does a double take as he sees Ginge sitting there. Oh yes, the Ginge test. As rough as she is looking now, she is still gorgeous. Once any would be boyfriends see her all is lost to me. I fade into the wallpaper when she is around and this is no exception as he is transfixed, well hard luck she has a boyfriend!

Oh no, I forgot James hasn't seen her either. I look over at him and he gives me a lovely smile. He really is so gorgeous and appears to be dealing with all of this rather well.

Just then Mr Watson, the chair of the resident's association pokes his head through the front door.

"Excuse me, officer, I am Ian Watson, of the Parkmead resident's association, do we need to evacuate the premises? If so, I will instigate the full fire drill."

Rob looks confused and I can't believe it, does the whole world need to know that I stayed out all night? Mum pipes up.

"No need love, all is fine, Maddie just spent the night with her new boyfriend and we thought that she had been abducted, but as you can see it is fine now."

MUM!! Could this be any more embarrassing? I pray that I am in some sort of weird dream and will wake up back at James's flat.

Suddenly, Mum decides to take charge of the situation.

"Right everyone I will make us all a nice cup of tea. Rob invite your colleagues in for one too, although I am not sure if we have enough mugs. Darren run and get yours and some milk, oh and you had better text Maddie's boss and tell her no need for the all staff email, she is fine and will be at work tomorrow as planned."

"You texted Betty?" What is this about an all staff email?"

"Yes Dear, Darren thought that we should inform them so that they could notify everyone around the country in case we needed a search party. Their customers and reps could spread the word and report any sightings back."

James now looks like he is going to explode with laughter. What on earth must he think of all this? I wouldn't blame him if he was well and truly put off me after this.

Ok enough is enough. They must all leave now!

"Look, everyone, thank you so much for your concern, but as you can see all is well. Mum, Dad I am sorry to have caused you so much worry, please go home and have a rest and I will call you in the morning. Rob, you had better go as you are obviously at work and I don't want to keep your colleagues waiting downstairs. Thank you for being concerned, I really do appreciate it you know. Darren, as you can see, I was not abducted but thank you for being such a good neighbour and worrying about me. I am sure that you will be rewarded by God for your concern."

"Oh Darren, you had better call the Vicar and let him know." Mum pipes up.

The Vicar! What's he got to do with it? I look at Darren who once again looks as if he wants the floor to open up and swallow him.

"Oh yes, they said prayers and lit candles for your safe return at Church today. At least they were answered."

I sit down heavily next to James. This is all too much. My father suddenly looks at me and then explodes into the loudest laughter that I have ever heard. It is so infectious that everyone joins in, except for Ginge, what is going on with her?

Tears are running down my father's face and suddenly the humour of the situation overtakes everyone. After a while, he composes himself and comes over and hugs me.

"Glad you're safe, little one. I'll drag your mother away and give you some space. Come on everyone let's leave them alone, it's been one hell of a day."

In no time at all, they have gone leaving James, Ginge and I sitting there in shock.

I look at her and say,

"Ginge are you ok? Something's obviously wrong."

She stands up and comes over with tears streaming down her cheeks.

"Oh Maddie, I was so worried, I really need you, I couldn't bear it if anything ever happened to you. What would I do?"

Ok, a bit over dramatic even for Ginge. Something must be up.

James is looking concerned and then jumps up.

"Maddie, I had better leave you two alone. At least we have cleared up the mystery of the disappearing Maddie."

I smile weakly at him and get up to walk him to the door. Ginge says,

"I am so sorry, I am pleased to meet you James, please don't hold any of this against Maddie, she is truly fantastic."

James smiles at her and I notice with satisfaction that it is just a normal smile and not a 'God I wish I was with you instead,' sort of smile.

"I know she is, it's what I love about her."

LOVE! Ok, just a figure of speech but it makes me feel warm inside. Oh, I forgot I still have my short fur jacket on, maybe that's the reason.

I walk him to the door and he draws me to him and kisses me, I must take this Jacket off, I am definitely going to melt now.

"Maddie, what can I say, it's been - exciting. I will call you tomorrow, now get some rest."

I watched him leave, already looking forward to seeing him again.

As I go back inside, I can see the tears streaming down Ginge's cheeks.

"What is it Ginge? What's the matter?"

I put my arm around her and she sobs uncontrollably.

"It's Tommy; I think he has gone off me."

"Never! You must be mistaken. What's happened?"

"Well, we were having a lovely holiday at his home in LA. Then he gets a call from his mother. He seemed angry and then became really distant. He wouldn't talk to me about it and seemed to draw away from me. I spent the last few days virtually on my own and he never even dropped me off at the airport. He got me a cab saying he had commitments."

This doesn't sound good.

"Do you think that his mum said something that put him off you then?"

"She must have because everything was fine until then."

Once again, she starts crying.

"Ok Ginge, when are you due to see him again?"

"In two days', time, they are playing Miami and I'm booked on a trip there."

"Well cancel it, phone in sick or swap with someone else, you know what we need to do."

She nods looking at me sorrowfully. It is time for 72-hour lockdown.

"Hand me your phone," I say determinedly. Looking apprehensive she hands me her phone and I turn it off.

"Right, you get Elle and I'll get the Maltesers."

This is our relationship crisis summit. Normally it is for me, this is the first time that it's for Ginge as she has never been hurt before.

We cut all communication with the culprit for 72 hours and watch back to back inspirational DVDs while eating chocolate. The first step is Legally

Blonde 1 and 2, guaranteed to lift your spirits in a relationship crisis.

January 20th - Lockdown Lifted

Well, what a few days this has been. We have been well and truly inspired by our DVD collection. Ginge phoned in sick so missed the flight to Miami. I phoned in sick too, thinking how lucky it was that I could cite the emotional trauma of my kidnapping experience. Betty was very understanding for her and told me to come back when I was ready to and not before. I spoke to James and told him the situation; we have another date planned for Friday evening so he doesn't appear to have been put off me in the cold light of day.

I also texted Rob and thanked him for his concern, saying that I was sorry that it didn't work out but I hoped that we could be friends instead- ok a bit cliché but I do like his company.

Darren feels really bad about the whole abduction saga and keeps on leaving us supplies of past their sell-by date chocolate, largely in the form of last year's Easter Eggs.

Ginge is looking more like herself, although is still prone to the odd outburst and we can't watch anything connected to Rock Music or Italians.

Well, tomorrow I am back to work and then on Friday is my Date and I can't wait to see James again. In sympathy with Ginge, I have resisted the desire to talk about him nonstop, but it has been really hard as he is all that I can think about.

Ginge is off until next week when she is due to fly to Orlando. Lucky thing I could so do with a trip to The Magic Kingdom.

Just then there is a knock on the door. I look at Ginge but she shakes her head and shrugs.

It better not be Cardigan Darren; I am still angry with him despite the supply of chocolate.

I open the door and do a massive double take, there filling up the doorway in all his Rock Godliness is Tommy. He looks absolutely exhausted and looks like he has just come off stage. He is wearing a bandana around his dark unruly hair and leather trousers with a ripped t-shirt and leather jacket. I can just make out the beginnings of a tattoo on his chest and he completely fills the doorway with his considerably muscular frame.

His eyes lock on to Ginge standing behind me and as I turn, I can see her standing there a vision in her leggings and oversized sweatshirt, with tears streaming down her beautiful face. Why don't I look like that even some of the time? Even in heartbreak, she is a vision.

With two steps, he is inside and gathers her in his arms.

"Don't leave me, baby," he says over and over while almost crushing her with his immense physique.

Tears come into my eyes at the scene before me. How romantic. He must have flown thousands of miles to be with her. If that isn't love, I don't know what is?

I feel really awkward now. I am so in the way. They are just standing there clinging on to each other.

I slip outside; I'll go for a walk and give them some privacy.

As I head outside, I can see a black Range Rover with tinted windows in the visitor's bay. I knock on the window and the guy inside winds the window down.

"Are you with Tommy?" I ask him. He nods at me looking a bit unsure, I mean he probably thinks I'm a crazed fan or something.

"Would you like a cup of tea? They may be some time."

"Don't worry, honey; I'm used to hanging around. I'll just wait until he lets me know what's happening."

"Ok, if you're sure, but shout if you change your mind, it's flat 15."

I smile and head off around the block. I know, I'll ring James.

He answers on the second ring.

"Hi Maddie, are you ok?"

The sound of his voice is so comforting.

"Yes fine, just had to get out of the flat for a bit as Tommy has rocked up and they are sorting out their issues."

"Do you want to come over?"

"I would love to but I have to go back to work tomorrow, I can't have another late night."

"Well, I have just about finished here, how about if I meet you at The Haywagon for a meal? It's only 30 minutes from yours and then you won't be too late."

"Would you do that for me? I mean, won't it put you out?"

"Not at all, I would love to have dinner with you."

"Ok, then shall I see you at 8 pm?"

"I'll look forward to it."

I rush back towards the flat. The man is still waiting in his car, poor thing, I mean, how boring. I hope that he has a book to read.

I can hear Ginge and Tommy resolving their issues in Ginge's room, so decide to leave a note explaining my whereabouts.

Once ready, I make a mug of tea and grab some biscuits and head outside. Once I have deposited these to the grateful driver, I head off towards Richmond.

The Haywagon

I am beginning to love this place. James and I have had a lovely meal and once again the log fire is working its magic. We had a good laugh about our last date and how it ended and I filled him in on events with Ginge. It's getting late so we head outside to our relevant vehicles. James says, "Thanks again for an enjoyable evening, are you still ok to meet up on Friday?"

"Yes, what do you have in mind?"

"Well Jeremy has given me tickets for his Partner's play, it's called, Made in Montenegro."

He looks at me and I can see him smiling, obviously amused by the name.

"Doesn't sound very thrilling, does it?"

I feel disappointed; I would rather see Mamma Mia.

"Well we could check it out and grab a meal in Covent Garden if you want. You can stay over again, at the risk of seeing myself on Crimewatch."

I laugh and feel the excitement growing in me at the thought of seeing him again.

"I know, why don't you come to my office at say 7pm and we can go from there. That way I can finish what I have to do and I can show you where I work."

"Sounds good, but don't expect me to lend a hand with the photocopying or anything, because I charge a hefty hourly rate."

"Oh, do you now and what would that be, just in

case I need to ask?"

"Oh, let's say around £5000, but it would be no good anyway, because I don't like to mix business with pleasure."

He grins and grabs hold of me.

"Well Miss Brown, let me say, I would consider you worth every penny."

He kisses me and I feel the same sense of excitement as I did the first time. I can't wait for tomorrow night.

January 23rd - 6.30pm James's offices in Canary Wharf

Well, I made it here at last. I got the train as it's easier, although I absolutely hate getting the train! Nobody looks happy and there is always someone eating something really smelly in the carriage or somebody having a loud conversation on their mobile phone. In fact, most people seem glued to their phones these days, tapping away as if their life depended on it.

Today the person next to me was playing Candy Crush. I love it and am on level 289. It was with much satisfaction that I saw that they were only on level 101. I spent the rest of the journey feeling very superior, throwing them knowing looks when they failed the level. I was trapped on one level for 3 weeks once, but I never gave up.

As I exit the train, I realise that my bag is quite heavy as I have packed my things for my sleepover with James. The trouble is I am going to have to carry it everywhere now, I certainly didn't think this one through.

James's offices are very impressive. I head into the reception area which is very modern with lots of huge paintings and modern Art dotted around. The receptionist has long gone as it is obviously past the usual working hours.

Text to James
Hi, I'm at reception.
Where shall I go?
M xx

Text from James
Get the lift to level 8
Turn right, head to the end
Office in front of you
Xx

I hate lifts. I have a phobia that I will get stuck in them. I can't manage the stairs with this case though. Oh well onwards and upwards. The office is deserted. It is dark outside and I can see the lights outside twinkling in the darkness like little stars.

In front of me is James's office. It has his name on the door, although I don't know why? I am sure that his staff know it's his.

I knock and hear him shout, "Come in"

As I push the door open, I see that he is not alone. There is a stunning woman standing behind him. She has long dark hair and smouldering eyes. She flashes me a look of dislike as though annoyed by the interruption. She doesn't move and stays in her position bending down towards him flashing her considerable assets at the same time.

"Oh sorry, I didn't know you were in a meeting." I say feeling as though I have interrupted them. Smiling at me James jumps up and comes over to me. He hugs me and gives me a kiss much to the annoyance of his colleague.

"Maddie, meet Ava."

I smile although I don't feel much like smiling and say, "Hi, pleased to meet you." which is most definitely a lie. She doesn't say anything just stands there frostily.

"Ava and I are working on an exciting new project on a subject close to your heart," he says smiling warmly at me.

"What chocolate?" I say grinning.

"No Biscuits," says James triumphantly.

"Ava has a contact in the US who wants to break into the European market and needs an agency to manage the advertising and PR. They are accepting bids from various companies, so we have to put a solid proposition together and pitch the idea in a couple of months' time in New York." Goodness, this sounds big.

"That's great James; do you think you stand a good chance?"

Ava snorts as though I have said something funny and then she speaks in a cold voice to match her cold exterior. Gosh, I hope that she isn't doing the pitch, who would want her managing their account.

"My contact is very high up in the organisation and has assured me that our proposal will be very well received. It is just a formality, really."

James smiles again and I can see that he is very excited about this deal. He looks at Ava and says, "Sorry Ava, we will have to finish this on Monday. Maddie takes priority now and we have plans."

Inside I am doing a victory dance in front of Ava, my inner self making the loser sign at her; outwardly I appear calm and collected.

Ava looks really annoyed and says, "Of course James, I understand. Never mind it can wait until next week, we can work late until it is done."

She looks triumphantly at me as she leaves. I wonder if she has ever had the business not pleasure conversation.

11pm - Thames View Apartments

Ok, not all dates can go well. The show was ghastly. It was even more boring than I had first thought and it was really hard to stay looking entertained in front of Jeremy and his boyfriend, Felipe, who sat with us.

James was obviously finding it difficult too, and I had to keep on nudging him to prevent him from falling asleep. It seemed to last for hours but finally it ended and we quickly made our escape. We hadn't even had time to grab something to eat, and all we managed to find was a hot dog from a nearby stall. I really wanted two but didn't want to appear greedy.

We decided to head back as we were both tired. As we go inside, I am reminded once again of how lovely his flat is.

James heads to the kitchen and says, "I need a drink after that, would you like a glass of wine?"

"Thank you, James, just the bottle will be fine."

I say raising my eyes up and laughing. He grabs two glasses and the bottle and we head into the living room. Ok red wine and cream sofas don't go well with me. I sit anxiously on the settee. The view is amazing, yet another patio window overlooking the London skyline. James pours me a glass and sits down next to me. "Never again will I accept free tickets to something that I know nothing about," he grumbles.

I laugh and snuggle up next to him, thinking that it would have been much better to have stayed in instead.

As we sit there enjoying listening to the music that he has put on, I feel really at ease. Suddenly he looks at me with a serious expression and says, "Maddie, I know that we haven't known each other long but I feel so comfortable with you. I want you to know that I love spending time with you and hope that you would consider becoming my girlfriend."

Gosh, that's an unexpected speech. Do people officially ask others out these days? He is looking quite vulnerable and worried, so I stroke the side of his face and look into his eyes saying, "I would love that James. I can't imagine how I would feel if you were not around and I adore spending time with you."

We start to kiss and the mood has changed and turned much more serious. He stands up and says,

"Maddie, say no if you want to but I would really like to spend the night with you. We don't have to do anything just cuddle if you want."

I don't even need to think about this, I stand up and put my hand in his. "I would like nothing more."

January 24th - 10am

What a night. Put it this way James and I cuddled in ways that I didn't think possible!

We are now officially a couple in every way and it feels so right.

I couldn't have been happier to wake up beside him this morning. He is currently in the shower after our morning cuddle and then when we are ready, we have decided to have breakfast in bed. In fact, we may even have lunch here too. I'm not sure about dinner but you never know.

January 25th - 2pm

Ok, we are finally going to venture outside for a nice Sunday lunch before I head off home. We have certainly worked up an appetite!

February 5th

The last few weeks have been manic. My life has fallen into a pattern of work all week and then spending the weekends with James in London.

James is working very hard on the pitch for the American Biscuits and spends most evenings closeted in his office with Ava. I can cope with it though because my new best buddy Jeremy also can't stand her and has made it his mission to monitor their meetings personally.

Ginge is back to normal with Tommy, apparently, the reason was that his mother had called to say that his sister is getting married in May and he should bring his girlfriend. Tommy was worried that if Ginge met his family she would go off him - as if that's likely - and so distanced himself from her because he is ashamed of them and feared that once she met them, she wouldn't want to know him anymore.

I mean how bad can they be? Ginge may come from a wealthy family but she is not a snob. Apparently, he was frantic when she didn't show up the next time and when he couldn't reach her on her phone, he decided to jump on a plane to find her. He was so worried that he had driven her away and couldn't rest until he saw her again. How romantic!

Cardigan Darren is still angry with me for finding love, even though he is now in huge demand in the

Christian circles, for his new-found skill of massage. He is even thinking about giving up the Supermarket to expand his business, what will we do then for food?

I finally had my 1-1 and Betty went easy on me due to the trauma of my abduction - ok I know it wasn't true, but sometimes in life opportunities present themselves that are too good to ignore. It also helped that the Simpson's order came through and they have repeated already. The new Southampton store is still a little way off, but at least I have irons in the fire.

February 13th - Day before Valentines

What do you get your new boyfriend who already has everything on your first Valentine's Day? The shops are full of cards and gifts but none of it seems right somehow. Ginge is on tour with Tommy that night and has bought some sexy underwear and some pink fluffy handcuffs, that she is going to surprise him with after the concert. I would be far too embarrassed and knowing my luck, I would get locked into them after losing the key and have to be cut out by Fireman Rob and his cronies.

WHAT AM I GOING TO DO?

February 14th - Valentine's Day

Luckily, this year the 14th is on a Saturday, my date night with James. In a flash of inspiration, I decided to surprise him at work. I have packed a lover's picnic consisting of pink champagne, strawberries, chocolate and little sandwiches cut into hearts.

I am also wearing a really sexy dress under my fake fur coat and have pampered my body all week, so I am now seduction ready.

7pm - James's offices - Canary Wharf

I walk into the reception and once again it is deserted. I now know where to go, so head off into the lift. So far so good on operation Valentine's seduction surprise.

Gosh, this basket is heavy. Maybe I should have got one with wheels. I will be as red as a Valentine's Day heart at this rate.

His offices are also deserted; no doubt everyone is at home enjoying their Valentines shenanigans.

As I draw near to his office, I can hear raised voices inside. Oh no, he is arguing with someone. I had better wait outside, as I don't want to interfere with his business.

I sit at Jeremy's desk and wait. Jeremy doesn't appear to be a very tidy PA, there are papers everywhere. Something catches my eye; it looks like it could be the Biscuit Ad that they are working on. I can't help myself and my curiosity gets the better of me.

Flicking through the A3 colour sheets I can see that it is indeed the Biscuit presentation. Oh well, it's not as if I have rummaged around looking for it, I'll just cast my consumer eye over it.

7.20pm

This Ad is rubbish. It's all about aliens landing in Europe and bringing American biscuits with them. Whose idea was this? The main alien appears to be called, "Biscog" I mean, Really!!!

They can't really think that they are going to win anything other than a one-way ticket home with this. I bet its Ava's idea; James would never think that this would work in a million years. Maybe that's what they are arguing about.

7.25pm

Suddenly the door bursts open and Ava comes rushing out looking extremely annoyed. She sees me sitting there and manages to sneer at me as she passes. I can't imagine why James employs her. I wouldn't let her loose on any of my customers.

I'm quite nervous now, what if he shouts at me too?

I poke my head through the door and see him

standing by the window staring out at the city below. "James, are you ok?" He turns around and he looks tired and pre-occupied.

However, his face relaxes when he sees me and smiles as he races over and lifts me up into a bear hug. "God, I've missed you so much," he says raining kisses down onto me. Wow what a welcome, maybe he should argue with his staff more if this is what happens.

"Happy Valentine's Day," I say shyly and he looks at me in surprise.

"Oh, of course, it is, I almost forgot."

"I've got a surprise for you," I say trying to contain the disappointment that I am feeling as he has obviously forgotten.

"Oh, what is it?" he suddenly looks a bit worried.

"I have made us a Valentine's Day picnic that we can have in your office," I say triumphantly. "What here, are you sure? wouldn't you prefer a more romantic setting?"

"What could be more romantic than here? All I want is your company and we have the whole of London at our feet."

He grins and says, "Well, in that case, let me clear us a space."

He sweeps everything off his desk and hoists me up onto it so we are sitting there as if on a throne, looking out at the twinkling lights.

"James, the picnic is out there," I laugh and jump down to go and retrieve it.

As I come in I notice that he has turned off all the lights except for one creating a more romantic glow. He has also placed a package where I was sitting on the desk wrapped in black paper with a red ribbon around it.

"Happy Valentine's day baby," he says and comes and kisses me passionately.

"Oh, I thought that you had forgotten." I say grinning from ear to ear.

"How could I forget our first Valentine's day? You would never forgive me."

I take hold of the gift and gently remove the packaging. Inside is a black padded box and as I open it, it reveals a beautiful silver bracelet with a heart attached.

I can't help it and tears come into my eyes as I look at him. "Thank you, James, I love it and I love you too."

"Not as much as I love you," he answers and all thoughts of a picnic are out of the window, as we make full use of the privacy of James's office.

8.30pm

As we sit on the floor of James's office and devour the picnic, I suddenly remember the raised voices that I heard as I arrived.

"James when I got here, I didn't come in because I heard raised voices. Is everything alright?"

He looks startled and then the tension in his face comes flooding back, making me regret mentioning it. "Oh nothing, just work related."

"Is it the American Ad? Are things not going to plan?"

He sighs and I remember his policy on business and pleasure. However, he looks at me and says, "I am just not sure that I like the direction it is heading. Ava is very good at her job and comes highly recommended, but I think the Ad is wrong."

"Well make her change it then," I say with determination.

"You must trust your own judgement as it's your company after all."

"The trouble is she has insider knowledge about the client and has assured me that this is what he is looking for. It gives us a head start on the other bids and she believes that we could talk him around once the deal has been done."

I ponder on what he has just said.

"Can you do a second pitch with the idea that you think would be better?"

"No, we only get one shot. There are other companies in the frame and we get one go and then it's on to another one."

He pulls me close and says, "Anyway enough of

work don't let it interfere with our evening. Come on let's get back to the flat, I have a surprise waiting."

Wow another surprise, I can't wait.

9.30pm - Thames View Apartments

James has his hands over my eyes as we wait outside his front door.

"Now no peeking until we get inside," he says sternly.

I shake my head wondering what it could be. We go inside and he closes the door.

"Ok you can look now," he says excitement in his voice.

I open my eyes and I can't believe them, the whole apartment is covered in red roses, with candles twinkling on every surface. There are fairy lights strewn all over the place and he flicks a switch and romantic music fills the room. He leads me onto the balcony and we stand there swaying to the music while looking out over London.

"But how did you do all of this, I mean you have been at work?"

He laughs and says, "Well Jeremy has helped and I did most of it last night."

I can't believe how beautiful it all is, and that he has gone to so much trouble. I am really the luckiest girl in the world.

James leads me into the kitchen where there is champagne in an ice bucket on the side. He picks it up and leads me from the kitchen to the bedroom where there are rose petals strewn all over the bed.

Ok, just how much input has Jeremy had here? In fact, I half expect to see him hiding in the corner, ready to serenade us with a guitar.

James places the bottle by the side of the bed and gently undresses me, soon I am naked before him and he quickly joins me. Our lovemaking is so tender yet passionate. I can't seem to get enough of him and it appears he feels the same way.

We lay in each other's arms happy and content, taking turns in drinking from the champagne bottle. I couldn't be happier than at this moment. This is all I want, to be here next to the man I love, getting steadily drunk!

March 1st

Ginge is home, and we have decided to have a girly day shopping. I really miss her when she is gone and now that I am away most weekends, we barely see each other. This weekend James is away on business, so Ginge and I, can have a great time indulging in some retail therapy.

We get up nice and early and head off down the A3 towards our favourite outlet shopping experience.

In no time at all, we are there and on the escalators to retail happiness.

Even though I am totally in love with my boyfriend, even that pales into insignificance next to the buzz of a bargain. I mean what is there not to love?

There is the thrill of entering the shop, not knowing what you may find in the hallowed walls within. You look through the many rails and shelves, on the quest to find the perfect item that you absolutely cannot live without. It doesn't matter if you don't find it straight away, you just move on to the next shop, will it be there?

The tension builds as you take in the array of wares tempting you and then you find it, the Holy Grail, or in this case a pair of Timberland boots for £19, reduced from £90.

Hallelujah!

You absolutely must buy the item, because if you

falter and dither about it all is lost. I cannot count the times that I have decided not to purchase the aforementioned product, probably not sure that I actually need it. This is the moment of weakness that gets you in the end. On returning home all you can think about is what you have missed out on. Suddenly, every time you go to wear something, you think of it, realising just how much your wardrobe needed it. You try to find it online, only to discover that it is either twice the price or no longer available. You spend more time and money heading back to purchase it, only to discover that it has gone. All at once it is the single most important item in your life and you are devastated at its loss.

Shopping with a friend is also very tricky. When asked if they should purchase the item it is easy to encourage them to do so. If they buy more than you it makes you feel justified in your own retail abandonment. It's not your money after all, so who cares if the lime green, crochet vest top is hideous, it just makes you look like you have better taste and you can wander around feeling like a style goddess.

Well, Ginge and I have our shopping routine off pat and several hours later have purchased, three tops, two dresses, four sets of naughty underwear- well, you have to think of your partners, you can't forget them - two white fluffy towels, (bargain buy one get one free) two bottles of perfume, two handbags, one pair of previously mentioned Timberland boots and three t-shirts.

Right, halfway there, time for lunch.

We decide to eat at a well-known Italian restaurant, after a trip to the car to deposit our purchases and free up carrying space for round two.

Once we have ordered we indulge in our favourite pastime, talking about our boyfriends.

Ginge says, "Tommy is getting more and more worried as the wedding approaches. I keep on reassuring him, but it doesn't seem to make any difference. How bad can they be?" Suddenly a terrible thought crosses my mind.

"Oh, Ginge do you think they're -Trailer Trash?"

"It wouldn't bother me if they were; it's Tommy that I love. Anyway, how is James and is he still having to spend time with that ghastly Ava?"

I pull a face and shudder at the very mention of her name.

"Yes, it's quite full on at the moment. They are currently in New York on a fact-finding mission, as the deadline is approaching for the postal submissions. The actual presentation is at the beginning of May."

"Really? What dates?"

Ginge looks at me with an excited expression.

"I think it's the second week. They have to go to New York."

Ginge claps her hands in excitement.

"That's when Tommy's sister is getting married and it's in New York! Why don't you come with me and you can give me moral support, as well as James at the same time?"

That sounds great, but then my heart sinks.

"The trouble is Ginge, I don't think that James will want me to come, as he doesn't like to mix business with pleasure. He already has Jeremy and Ava with him."

"Oh, come anyway, pleeease. You can stay with us and think of the shopping that you could do in New York. I'll get you on a flight, so it won't cost anything."

Hmm, actually it does sound like fun and I am owed some holiday at work.

"Ok, great I'd love to, in fact, I may not mention it to James, as I don't want to stress him out any more than he is already."

Ginge smiles happily, and it's not just because our favourite pasta dish has arrived with the artisan bread basket.

Once we have devoured the food Ginge says,

"Oh, I almost forgot. Tommy's band is playing at the O2 next month and he says that he can get you tickets if you want. You can come backstage and everything. It would be really cool to show you life on the road."

Oh, my God, this is great. I nod enthusiastically and wonder if James is into Rock music. I know, I could buy him that great t-shirt I just saw, it has rocker stamped all over it.

Two hours later and we are through. Through all the shops and all of our money, for the next three months. Oh well, I can always return them if they don't fit. Actually, I very rarely do, they just live under the bed in their carrier bags.

We sing Rock songs all the way home, such is the natural high from our fabulous day out. I hope that Cardigan Darren is in to help us carry it all upstairs. Guiltily I think I should have bought him that cardigan I saw in the clearance section for £6.99. I mean he does feed us well after all, it's the least I could do.

March 11th

I stayed at James's last night as I have some appointments near to his flat. I love waking up with him and it's a real bonus when we see each other mid-week.

I even met Hatty Tatty. She isn't at all what I expected. I envisaged her like a mother hen type, probably middle-aged with four kids. Well, how wrong was I?!

Hatty Tatty is her business name. Her real name is, Harriet Tattershall. She can't be much older than I am and drives a sweet little smart car with, "Hatty Tatty, Domestic Goddess" written on the side. She has a good business set up and cleans for most of the apartments in the block. She combines cleaning with other services, such as shopping to order and social planning. She employs six people who also drive similar vehicles. Her husband is a city banker, so she doesn't have to work, but she loves her "Empire" as she calls it and is probably earning as much as he does out of it.

She turned out to be great fun and told me loads of stories about people leaving their flats empty and visiting them once a year to go to Harrods. No wonder property is so expensive in London.

I am heading along the South bank towards Tower Bridge. My first call is in Shad Thames and I love the little cobbled streets just off the river. I grab a coffee and drink it as I wander along. Actually, I wish I hadn't brought the full range with me, my suitcase is making a terrible racket on the cobbles, announcing my arrival to all and sundry. If I break a wheel, I will have to abandon it and say I was mugged, it's far too heavy to actually carry.

I think that I'll just take a seat on a nearby bench and drink my coffee and recover.

As I look around me, I look at all the people rushing by. London is so multicultural; it's like the League of Nations just along this stretch.

Hang on a minute; I think I see a familiar face. Squinting and feeling guilty about the ignored invitation to the free eye test, I try to focus.

Just over by the railings are two people, one older man wearing the most old-fashioned pinstriped suit and a BEARD! What is it about beards these days? With him looks to be the nightmare that is Ava!

Wow, I never knew she had a boyfriend. They are all over each other; it's quite revolting to watch. Quickly I take a photo and message Jeremy.

Snap Chat to Jeremy

Who's playing away from the Office today?

Text from Jeremy

That can't be Ava, she's seeing a client in North London. She must have a double!

Text to Jeremy
Looks a lot like her though. Are you sure?

Text from Jeremy.
I'll call her and if she answers We'll know!

Text from Jeremy
It's gone to voicemail. typical. Can you follow them, Miss Marple?

Text to Jeremy
Sorry, I'm late for my call. I could walk past them though.

Text from Jeremy
Go on, I dare you!

Ok, never one to run from a challenge, I stand up and grab my case. I walk towards them; however, before I can get to them, they walk away in the direction that I am going.

What do I do now? I can't run after them, not least because I have this heavy case rattling around behind me. They have their arms around each other and I cannot see their faces.

It's not long before they disappear down a side road. Bother! Now we will never know for sure.

I would have loved it to be her and see her face when she saw me, huh, try explaining that meeting to James.

My phone buzzes.

Text from Jeremy
Well??

Text to Jeremy
Lost them!!!

It's made me think though. What if it was Ava? Why would she be meeting her boyfriend when she was supposed to be at work?

March 29th - Easter Sunday

I couldn't avoid it any longer. Mum has been on and on at me to invite James around for dinner. So far, I have resisted but now its Easter I couldn't get out of it.

I have briefed him on what he may expect but it is still with trepidation that I ring their doorbell.

The door flies open and there is Mum in all her Easter glory. She is wearing a Rabbit apron with those Bunny Ears on an Alice band.

"Maddie! James! Happy Easter, come in, come in."

I hand her the Easter eggs and Daffodils that I have brought with me and with a sigh follow her in. She says excitedly,

"Let me take your coats and get you a drink. Stewart, get them a drink and make it a large one."

My Dad nods, grinning at me as he carries out her command.

James smiles at me reassuringly; I mean, I have only been going on about this for the last month ever since Mum said,

"And don't even think about not coming to us for Easter."

I have well and truly moaned about it, despite his constant reassurances that it won't make any difference to our relationship at all, even if my parents are from the nuttier side of the tree - and that's saying something!

I groan as I take in the scene before me. Mum has taken full advantage and invited almost every member of my family, who are shoehorned into the living room like sardines in a tin.

The room is decorated for the occasion with various Easter paraphernalia; there are Easter egg hunt signs and garlands of bunnies and lambs, alongside the traditional Easter tree, dominating a large table groaning under the weight of a chocolate-fuelled banquet. She has even managed to find a chocolate fountain, with marshmallows on sticks made to look like bunnies. Mum calls everyone to attention and says,

"Right everyone, now that the happy couple is here, we can begin."

I cringe; she makes it sound like it's our wedding. I know that she is doing it on purpose, dropping in wedding-related descriptions into everyday conversation. No prizes for guessing what her secret wish is.

"Mum, aren't we going to Church for the Easter service?" I say wickedly, knowing immediately what her answer will be.

"Oh no, dear, we simply haven't got the time. There is too much to do here."

Oh no, the true meaning of Easter doesn't lie in the hallowed walls of the Church in my mother's eyes, it lies in the garden in the form of an Easter egg hunt!

She thrusts ribbon festooned baskets at us and we all head outside.

It has been raining, and the grass is soggy. There is also a big black thunder cloud overhead, and it is freezing. James and I trudge around the postage stamp sized lawn in search of hidden treasures - in this case in the form of Cadbury's crème eggs.

I am a bit concerned about James. He has been working late, not just on the Biscuit project; he also has other campaigns on the go and is inundated.

He is such a control freak and refuses to delegate the workout, insisting on creative control of everything. I sort of understand where he is coming from though; I wouldn't want anyone near my customers either.

We find about five and then I can bear it no more. We head inside for some hot chocolate.

Note to Self: Give up chocolate post-Lent!

I've never been very disciplined at abstinence. My trick was always to give up something I already hated like chickpeas!

I turn to James who is bearing up valiantly and say,

"How long do you think we should stay without appearing rude?"

He laughs at me and replies,

"Come on Maddie, where is your Easter spirit? We have a feast awaiting us which would be rude to ignore."

"Yes, and a heart attack for dessert, judging by this lot."

After we have spoken to every member of the family, who for some reason keep on nudging us, winking and patting their noses, as though they have a secret that they do not want to divulge. James looks confused, are we missing something?

We decide to head off using James's demanding work schedule as an excuse but are really just desperate to get back to the flat. It would appear that all the melted chocolate has given us a much better idea of how we want to spend Easter.

April 11th - Crash & Burn

At last! Tonight's the night. We are heading off to the O2 to Tommy's concert. I am so excited. We have backstage passes and Tommy is sending a Limo to pick us up!!!

James stayed here last night, which was a bit strange after the luxury of his apartment. We only have one bathroom and the kitchen is so small it would fit inside his much-coveted walk-in wardrobe. It is so wasted on a boy! If I had it there would be large floor to ceiling mirrors with lights around them. Lots of beautiful fancy boxes, containing gorgeous shoes and hats. Drawers that pull out, housing all sorts of lingerie and accessories; not to mention the shelves holding a vast array of cashmere jumpers and rails groaning under designer dresses. Half of his is taken up with scuba diving gear. I mean, how many times has he gone scuba diving in the River Thames? None actually, what a waste!

Ginge also stayed last night despite Tommy pleading with her to join him at his luxury 5* Hotel. She said she needed the rest as she had just flown in that morning and it would be one hell of a night tonight.

Cardigan Darren is also coming with a DATE! I am almost more excited about that than the concert. Please don't let it be Miss Cardigan! He even bought a new cardigan for the occasion. He proudly showed it to us yesterday. It is black with leather look sleeves. I feel so proud.

We ordered Pizza for energy and are waiting for the others to join us. I have resurrected my Rock Rebel look and totally look the part. James is wearing the Rocker t-shirt that I bought for him and his jeans and a leather jacket. We are proudly wearing our backstage passes around our necks on lanyards.

Ginge suddenly makes her entrance and we bow down before her. I don't even want to look at James to see his expression, as I probably won't like what I see.

She is a vision, in a figure-hugging black dress, with silver chunky jewellery. Her hair is loose and flowing around her like spun gold. I would absolutely die to look like that and feel instantly depressed. Then I feel a hand in mine and turn to see James looking at me and smiling. He bends towards me and kisses me making my heart flutter.

He squeezes my hand again and pulls me near to his side. I may not look like a supermodel, but I wouldn't trade James for any of it.

The doorbell rings and it is with great excitement and anticipation, that we open the door to reveal Cardigan Darren and his date.

I can't believe it! His date is not at all what I expected. She is a tall - and I mean TALL! - slim girl of about 21, with long curly brown hair and beautiful green eyes. She is wearing cutoff jeans which make her legs look even longer and a crochet vest top, with hippy fringing and some great chunky jewellery. Darren is also transformed. He has gelled his hair so that it is spiky at the front and even his cardigan looks cool.

"Hi everyone," he says proudly.

"Meet Desdemona."

Wow, even a cool name, where on earth did he meet her?

We all rush forward and say hi. It turns out that they met at Massage College, or whatever you call it. Dessie, as he calls her was blown away by his charm and they have been dating for one month already. How could I not have known all this? I feel bad; I know that I have been wrapped up in my own love life, but even so!

Apparently, they were paired up in the class to practice on each other; well it appears that the stories are true about massage leading on to other things. Remind me to never let Darren practice on me.

Soon we are in the Limo and I can hardly contain my excitement. I have never ridden in one before and feel like a film star. It will take us about an hour to get there and the bar is stocked with champagne and all manner of other drinks and nibbles.

This is the life!

I really want to poke my head out of the large sunroof like you see them do in the Hollywood movies. The trouble is, it's raining and my hair would then take up the whole Limo, we are also on the M25 which is not as exotic as Hollywood.

We are having so much fun, Darren is a changed man and both he and Dessie give us neck and shoulder massages all the way. Actually, I can see why Darren is in such demand now.

Fully relaxed, after consuming the mini bar and after our massages, we arrive at the O2.

We can see the concert goers staring at the car as we drive in, probably hoping that it is the Band. We are taken to the VIP entrance and stagger out like true Rock groupies.

I feel like I'm in Wayne's world and want to hold out the passes in front of me as I cut through the crowd. I resist the urge, however, as I try to stay cool.

We are now officially backstage and my excitement is at fever pitch. I look wildly around but all I can see is equipment and strange people milling around. I don't recognise anyone famous, are we even in the right place?

I nudge Ginge and say,

"Ginge where is everybody? I don't see anyone I recognise yet."

Ginge laughs, "You won't see anyone here. The

band get delivered by helicopter, 5 minutes before the show and the other invited guests will be in the special room overlooking the stage where food and drink are laid out. Come on we'll head on up there."

Disappointed at the lack of depraved rock chicks and rockers littering the back-stage area, we follow Ginge to the VIP room. There is a bouncer on the door who smiles at Ginge and says, "Hi Ginny Baby, your home town this week, how does it feel?"

"Great thanks Mario," Ginge replies.

"Is it a good turnout?"

He nods and says,

"If anyone gives you any trouble just let me know. No one is too famous to get thrown out."

Ginge laughs and says, "I'll bear that in mind."

Ginge has told me before that Mario is employed to look after the girlfriends of the band members. They are often hit on by the other guests, normally other rock stars and people from the music industry. Pete, the lead singer is going out with Marcia a Playboy Bunny and Nico's girlfriend is a well-known model. Rocky's girlfriend is his childhood sweetheart Ester. Ginge is the most normal one, although I think the prettiest, but then I am biased.

Maybe I shouldn't have invited James, once again I feel very inadequate.

The room is packed and there is a lot of squealing as Ginge is surrounded by her rocker friends. Ginge pulls us over to meet them, they seem nice enough but we soon leave them to it.

James and I stand back and take in the surrounding scene.

I am sure that I can see many famous faces here. I wish that I could take pictures but there is a strict, no camera, policy. I can see why as I spy that prim and proper weather girl from Breakfast TV, being less than prim and proper with the news presenter. I am sure that he is married to someone else, when will these celebrities ever learn?

The noise in the arena is deafening. We grab some VIP drinks from the VIP bar and head towards the window overlooking the stage. The place is packed and the lights and stage are amazing. There is loud music playing and the fans are getting well and truly in the mood for the concert.

I absolutely love their music. It stirs my soul and I have every album they've made - ok, Ginge gave them to me, but I would have bought them if she hadn't.

I can see Darren and Dessie absorbed in each other in the corner. I can't get used to seeing him with a girl, especially a hot one like Dessie. I am happy for him though.

James holds onto my hand and grins at me. He is obviously enjoying himself and I am glad as he has had such a difficult couple of months.

Then the lights dim and the anticipation grows. The

arena erupts as the band explodes onto the stage, to the opening bars of their latest hit. The noise levels are through the roof. There are no dancers or backing singers, just the band belting out their hits and playing their drums and guitars like extensions of their manhood.

God, they are so hot! Or is it just the leather look jacket making me sweat?

We are all dancing and singing as if our lives depended on it, punching the air and gyrating as though we are part of some strange Rock Cult.

Mario is quite busy throwing people out of the VIP bar. Should I feel annoyed that someone hasn't tried it on with me yet?

We watch the masses from our vantage point. Everyone is singing and dancing and some are even crowd surfing, trying to get to the stage. Security is tight though and as soon as they reach it, they are whisked away by the security guards, who form a line in front of the stage, like riot police.

Mental Note: Add Crowd surfing to Bucket List.

Ginge is having a great time singing and dancing along to the music. She must do this every week, but she still appears to relish it.

The songs are great. Tommy writes all the songs, and he is very talented. The band have been together since High School and have worked their way up through the bars and clubs until they were signed by a record label. Their feet haven't touched the ground since and they are very much at the top of their game and in huge demand. Their concerts sell out within minutes and they are constantly asked to appear in various shows and events.

Tommy just loves to write and perform and Ginge says that the celebrity side of it doesn't appeal to him much. He turns most invitations down and prefers to spend his spare time at his house in LA, writing more songs and chilling out with Ginge.

Then I hear the opening bars of the song that I know that Tommy wrote for Ginge. I look over at her and she is transfixed watching him with a faraway look in her eyes.

Tommy sings this one and fixes his gaze on the VIP area, although I am sure that he can't see her from there. He is obviously singing it to her and tears form in my eyes as I watch them.

I do sort of know what it is like after I went on holiday with my parents to the Haven holiday site in Dorset. There was a karaoke contest and some nerdy guy sang, "Keep on loving you," by REO Speedwagon and looked at me the whole time. It made me feel really uncomfortable, especially as everyone thought that we must be together and the really hot guy that I had my eye on thought so too.

James squeezes my hand, and I put my head on his

shoulder. He may not be an International Rock star, but I wouldn't swap him for the world.

Two hours later and the concert has finished. The band have dashed off stage and we grab our things and head back-stage once again.

I turn to Ginge and say, "Are we going to meet up with Tommy now?"

She nods enthusiastically.

"Yes, but not here, they will have gone by now. They leave before the masses by helicopter. The Limo is going to take us to their hotel for a post-concert party."

We are now very excited. Partying with Rock stars in their hotel. Who would have thought!

The London Hilton - 12.00pm

It's taken us ages to get here, due to the large amount of traffic from the show. I can see why they take the helicopter.

The hotel is very posh and there are lots of people milling around, despite the late hour.

We are shown to a large room, which is already full of people. There is loud music blaring out from somewhere and a large table of food laid out.

As we push through the crowd, I notice lots of our fellow VIP's are here already. I can see the Playboy

Bunny, locked on to her band member boyfriend.

Ginge suddenly squeals and rushes forward, straight into the arms of Tommy, who is lounging against a wall at the end.

Well, there will be no conversation from them for a while!

Darren, Dessie, James and I grab some drinks and sit down on a nearby settee taking in the scene. It is wall to wall, leather and denim. There are people snogging everywhere and lots of drunken shouting and arguing. I watch out for any famous faces, fascinated by the events in the room.

Just then Ginge pushes her way towards us, towing Tommy behind her.

"Hi, guys," he says.

"Thanks for coming, did you have a good time?"

Goodness, he is rather gorgeous, they are very well suited. I answer for everyone and say, "Yes it was great, thanks for the tickets and the Limo, we really appreciate it."

The others add their thanks and we squash up so that they can sit down.

Ginge plonks herself on to Tommy's lap and he plays with her hair, while we sit there chilling out.

Tommy is actually really funny and once we were over the awkwardness of sitting with somebody so famous, we all got on rather well.

Ginge whispers to me,

"Maddie, I'm staying here with Tommy tonight, as you know, but the Limo will take you back whenever you want, it's waiting outside. Don't go yet though, this party may last all night."

People keep on stopping to talk to Tommy and I am well and truly star struck. There are people here that normally just live in the magazines that I buy. It isn't right that they are real people. I had quite a chat with the presenter of the property programme that I love; she was totally on my wavelength and gave me some great tips on where the next property hotspot was likely to be.

James was having fun too; he spent ages talking to a well-known footballer, who plays for the team he supports. I think he gave him his business card, and the guy said that he would put him on the guest list for the next Home game.

Talking about business cards, Darren and Dessie were handing theirs out like confetti. I would never have thought that my revenge in church would have had such fantastic results. It was Darren who benefited from Divine Inspiration that day and not me.

Soon he will be, Cardigan Darren, masseuse to the stars. He may even have to move to Hollywood.

3am

I am well and truly done in. Ginge left about an hour ago with Tommy and Darren and Dessie have fallen asleep on the comfy couch. James pulls me up and we shake the massage twins awake and head outside to our waiting Limo.

Thank God for Limos! We all stretch out and fall asleep and before long are back at Parkmead. Now I know why they are called "Stretch Limos". What a night!

April 24th - Thames View Apartments

James and I are getting ready for some charity dinner that he has been invited to. It's only a couple of weeks until he flies to New York for the presentation, so I haven't seen much of him since the concert.

He is getting more and more anxious as the weeks go on and is quite short-tempered, probably because he is tired. I am hoping that a night out with make him relax.

As we get ready, I make the mistake of bringing up the subject of Ava and the Ad again.

"James, did you ever change the advert for the biscuit presentation?"

He looks cross and snaps,

"Of course not, I've told you Ava has it covered."

Not willing to give up I carry on.

"Well, I don't trust her. I am sure that she is not what she seems. I am convinced it was her that I saw that day in Shad Thames, when she was supposed to be in North London. You should be careful, you know. I think you should have a backup plan."

Ok, I supposed I asked for it as I pushed him when

he was already stressed, but James explodes.

"For goodness' sake Maddie, will you get over your obsession with Ava? She knows what she's doing and your constant bitching isn't helping. This is precisely the reason why I don't mix business with pleasure. I want to forget about work for 5 minutes, but you won't even give me that."

He storms out of the room and shaking I sit down in the nearby chair. Well, this is going to be a fun night.

7.30pm - Charity Gala Night at the Dorchester

Well, we got here, but the atmosphere is still subzero. We never argue so it is quite uncomfortable. We both looked out of the windows in the cab on the way here, not quite sure what to say.

When we arrive, we are shown to a big round table covered in a starched white tablecloth and sit down. Our table is filling up with various people from the world of Advertising. James knows most of them but I know nobody.

A pleasant looking man sits down next to me who turns out to be the Managing Director of a well-known sports clothing company. We have a good old conversation about the current trends and after 3 red wines, I feel more relaxed.

James has also relaxed and is laughing and joking with a rival.

I really need to go to the Ladies so excuse myself and head off to find them.

Why is there always a queue at the Ladies but never one at the Men's? I am so desperate; I decide to use the disabled one. I am sure that nobody will need it; if there is someone waiting as I exit, I will fake a limp, that has always worked in the past.

Luckily, I get away with it. She who dares wins! And I walk back into the large room.

Suddenly I stop dead in my tracks.

There is beardy man, with his arm around the same woman, who I am convinced is Ava. Huh, let's see what James has to say about this? I will prove to him, once and for all, that I am not mad.

Before I can get to there, James approaches them with a smile on his face and his hand outstretched. I saunter up to them smugly; wait until I tell him this is the same man that I only mentioned a few short hours ago.

The trouble is though, as they turn around, I notice that the woman is not Ava, but a very near copy of her. Damn! I was wrong, best not mention it now.

"Maddie, come and meet Quentin Brown and his lovely wife Rosemary," James says.

We all smile and shake hands and James says,

"Quentin is one of my rivals for the biscuit contract.

We will be competing against each other in New York, so don't give anything away."

They all laugh, but I don't think it's a natural laugh; it all seems quite forced, really.

Before we can chat further, the compere calls everyone to their seats for the meal and subsequent charity auction.

The food is lovely and I wonder how much a ticket costs to one of these events. Leaning over I say, "James, are the tickets expensive for one of these events, I could get one for my Mum and Dad for their anniversary."

James smiles and his eyes crinkle up - thank God, I am forgiven.

"£500 each." He says and arches his eyebrows.

"Oh, Ok, on second thoughts, they would probably prefer a Garden Centre voucher."

HOW MUCH?! We haven't even bid on anything yet. I had better not drink any more wine, I may get carried away and blow a year's salary.

I pick up the brochure for the charity auction and have a look at what's on offer. There are some really great things in here. There are the usual spa breaks and adrenaline-fuelled activities, but what takes my fancy are things like the diamond-encrusted Cartier watch, the designer handbag and the shopping experience in Paris, with flights and accommodation thrown in.

A bit disappointed not to see a trolley dash around Harrods listed as one of the items.

Note to self: Approach organisers and suggest item for next year's auction.

It soon begins and I look at James sitting there casually taking it all in. I forgot to ask him if he was going to bid for anything. The most I can do is buy a raffle ticket for the Fortnum and Mason Hamper; even they are £25 each.

I am amazed at the bids. They run into the tens of thousands of pounds. Our last Christmas raffle at Scentastic only raised £350 for the local hospice and the first prize was a Kindle. I know it's all for charity, but it is starting to make me feel quite ill. Money means nothing here. They are bidding per item more than I earn in a year. My inadequacies are very much to the surface now and I sink lower and lower into my seat.

James looks at me and smiles, he reaches out and takes my hand and then turns his attention back to the proceedings.

The next item is a holiday, with first-class flights, to Necker Island. The bidding starts and there is a lot of interest. I crane my neck to see who each of the bidders are and notice with surprise beardy man well and truly bidding for it.

It gets to £40,000 and the bids are drying up. Beardy is looking very pleased with himself and then before I know what is happening, my hand is flying in the air to indicate a bid of £42,000. WHAT?!!

I have obviously lost control of my limbs because I can see my hand in the air, but I don't know how it got there. Stunned, I look over at James, who is laughing at me, as he propels my hand upwards again for a bid of £45,000 against beardy.

"James, what are you doing?" I hiss at him.

"I can't afford this, I'll be arrested."

He laughs and thrusts my hand upwards again at £47,000.

I try to break free, but his grip is too strong. He winks at me and then once again holds my arm aloft as the bid reaches £50,000. The room is silent as the people watch this bidding war unfold. Beardy is not looking so pleased now and in fact is looking quite sick; obviously his male pride has got in the way of his common sense.

After what seems like forever, the hammer comes down and we have won a trip to Necker Island, for up to 6 people for £60.000.

Everyone claps and I just sit there looking stunned. James looks very pleased with himself.

"James, what have you done? You know you need to pay them the money, are you mad?"

"Possibly, but I happen to think that it's worth every penny. Six people making it £10.000 each. Bargain!"

Well, I'd hardly call it that; doesn't he remember that I can get us free flights on friends and family?

The rest of the evening passes in a blur. People keep on coming up to us and congratulating us on our winning bid. I still can't take it in and can't wait to get out of here and back to the real world.

Soon we are on our way and I turn my back on the weirdest experience of my life -so far, anyway.

May 2nd

It's the last weekend before James leaves for New York and we have decided to spend a quiet one at his flat. I still haven't told him that I am going too; I just mentioned that I was going on a trip with Ginge while he was away. When he asked me where, I lied and said that she was on standby, so we wouldn't know until the day before. Luckily, he knows nothing at all about how rostering is done on an Airline, so accepts my word.

We decide to get a takeaway and have it on his balcony overlooking the River Thames.

"I am really going to miss you, James, I hope that it all goes well for you," I say mid-mouthful. This Chinese takeaway is fab!

"Me too baby, I wish you were coming with me. We could take in the sights afterwards and make a week of it."

I am now confused; did I get this all wrong?

"Really James, I didn't think that you liked to mix business with pleasure."

"Oh, I don't but once the business is over the pleasure aspect could begin."

He grins at me with that cheeky grin that I love.

What do I do? Should I tell him that I'm going to be

there and we could meet up if he wants to, or would he be annoyed that I never said anything in the first place? I am so confused. Then I have a brainwave.

"You never know James, I might still make it to New York, as Ginge doesn't know where she is going yet, so who knows?"

"Fingers crossed then."

Suddenly I cheer up; well this trip may turn out even better than I first thought.

James looks at me and says,

"Maddie, I was thinking, we have never been to my house in Dorset and I would love to show it to you. Do you think that we could go there the weekend after I get back? Work could take a back seat for a couple of days and I think you will really like it there."

I nod excitedly, "I'd love to, thanks."

I had wondered why James hadn't invited me to his house in Dorset. He talks about it so much but hardly seems to spend any time there. I am intrigued to see it, as it's a part of his life that I know nothing about. I know that his parents live near there and even though I have spoken to them on the phone, I have never met them. I don't think that he is ashamed of them like Tommy, but apparently, they are always on holiday. Oh no, maybe it's me he's ashamed of! I hadn't thought about that possibility.

May 4th

James has now officially left for New York, with Ava and Jeremy in tow. Ginge and I are due to fly out tomorrow and Tommy's sister's wedding is a few days later.

It's been so busy at work lately; I am looking forward to the rest.

I have spent the day packing and make sure that I pack lightly so that I can get all my American shopping purchases back in my suitcase. I have changed my money into Dollars and filled out my visa online, so I am ready for the off.

May 5th - Gatwick Airport 8am

Once I had checked in Ginge showed me the way to the First-Class Lounge in the terminal. She then had to check in herself and I was left to my own devices.

I love it in here. I can eat and drink whatever I want for nothing and am always offered a complimentary spa treatment. You would never know that they have a hot tub here in the terminal, would you?

I decide on a full English breakfast and a manicure and pedicure. I look with interest at the other residents of the lounge. They are a mixed bunch of all ages and nationalities. I notice a man staring at me as I lounge; he smiles and raises his glass in the air towards me. Good God, I hope he doesn't think I'm a lady alone and therefore fair game. You hear all sorts of stories about businessmen on trips away. Well, this girl is not interested in joining the Mile-High club on this flight that's for sure. I look away hoping that he is not on my flight, it would be just my luck that he's sitting in the pod next to me.

Actually, I'm getting a bit bored now with all of this pampering and free food. I decide to head outside and hit the shops. I need a good selection of celebrity magazines and copious amounts of sweets for the journey. I may even buy a packet of biscuits and raise them in a good luck salute to James with my tea.

After I have sprayed loads of perfume and bought myself a rather flattering scarf, I head to the bookshop to join the long queue before we board.

There is no sign of Bill and his wheels, so I must walk to the gate. Goodness, you would think that if one travels first class, they would have a secret tunnel to the plane, or at least a Golf cart to transport you there.

Note to self: Write a letter to the chief executive of the airline, with the secret tunnel suggestion. Request free first-class seats for life as payment for the idea.

Once I am at the gate, I sit down and wait. The flight looks very busy and there are masses of people piling into the gate area. I am grateful that I have a friend on the flight who has upgraded me. The thought of sitting in economy, with someone kicking the back of my seat all the way to America fills me with dread.

I always seem to get a seat by the toilets as well. There is nothing worse than inhaling that stench for six hours each way.

The flight is called and Upper-Class passengers are called first. Smugly, I pick up my baggage and wheel it towards the tunnel. They don't know that I am flying for free and I don't care to let them know either.

Once I get on board, I see Ginge who shows me to

my seat.

"I'll try to get some time to chat, but we are quite busy at first." she says and then heads off to look after her passengers.

I am sitting in a little pod of my own and cannot see the person next to me. It is great, total privacy, cocooned in my own little world with someone to bring me food and beverages every so often.

I study the inflight magazine to check out the films on offer on my personal entertainment system.

Another Stewardess brings me a preflight Champagne. I smile and thank her and sit back in my chair looking out of the window at the activity on the ground below.

The flight is about six hours and I am too excited to think about sleeping.

The thought of staying at Tommy's is exciting; to see how a real-life Rock Star lives is not a normal everyday occurrence. I am prepared to be shocked!

Once everyone is on board, the cabin doors close and we push back. Time for Takeoff, my favourite part.

As we taxi out I think of James already there and hope that it goes well for him, although I doubt it if they stuck with "Biscog".

Soon we are airborne and once the seat belt signs are off, it seems that the whole of the cabin gets up to stretch their legs. I always find this a bit strange;

it's almost like a starting pistol, first off the blocks wins. Deliberately I stay where I am; you could never accuse me of following the crowd.

Ginge stops by with some more Champagne. I wish that she could sit with me and then we could talk all the way to the Big Apple.

I decide to watch a movie and choose the latest Disney film. It's the best chance I get these days, as I don't have any young friends to take to see them at the cinema.

Halfway through, the meal arrives and I balance it on the lap tray in front of me, while still enjoying the film.

Ok, it's been 2 hours now and I am getting bored with my own company. Time to stretch my legs.

I go in search of Ginge and find her serving behind the Bar in the centre of the cabin.

I sit at a stool to chat with her and she gives me another drink and some nibbles to munch on.

There are only three other people sitting there, one man on his own reading some report or another and an older couple wearing matching jumpers.

Why do couples do this? It's bad enough when you see mothers and daughters out shopping with each other in identical outfits, that I can sort of understand, but why do couples want to dress the same? If James turned up in the same outfit as me, I would be really put off.

"Hey Ginge, have you had your break yet?" I say as she busies herself tidying up.

"No, mine isn't for an hour yet. When I can get away, we can have a chat in the crew area if you like. Oh, by the way, have you heard from James yet? Do you know if he got there ok?"

"Yes, he texted me this morning and said that they were there and were going to be putting the finishing touches to the presentation today."

"Is that bitch Ava with him?"

"Yes unfortunately, at least Jeremy is there too, so he will let me know any gossip. What about Tommy? Has he said anymore about his family?"

Ginge pulls a face.

"He is still really stressed about the whole thing. No matter how many times I reassure him he is still on edge."

"They must be really bad for it to affect him this much."

She nods and then we hear a loud voice shouting and the sound of someone clicking their fingers.

"Waitress, Waitress! Hurry up, the service on this flight is appalling."

Ginge frowns and all of us at the Bar area look around to see a very smart woman, clicking her fingers at Ginge and frowning. Ginge hurries over despite the woman being so rude, more to avoid a scene than to placate the rude woman.

I shake my head and say, "Well I wouldn't want to be in her shoes."

The couple and the man look at me questioningly. The lady says in an American accent, "Why honey? Surely, she must be used to dealing with rude passengers. I'm not saying I agree with the woman's behaviour, but I am sure she is just one of many, isn't that right Brad?"

Her husband nods. "Yes, we see this all the time. People leave their manners behind at check in on these flights. Disgraceful if you ask me."

I shake my head and smile at them knowingly.

"Oh no, it's not Ginge's shoes that I am talking about, it's the rude woman's."

They look confused.

"Well, it's like this. Up here the cabin crew hold all the cards. You may think they are here just to serve the passengers and attend to their every whim. but they are really here for safety. If you upset the crew, they have ways of making you pay."

I now have their full attention.

"Well, there was this one time when the Captain of the plane was being extremely rude to the stewardess assigned to look after him. He spoke to her badly and messed her around. After that, there wasn't a drink that she gave him that wasn't tampered with in some way. She emptied the passenger's dregs into his cup and topped it up with fresh. She made up his meals with the leftovers from the trolleys and sneezed over his complimentary toothbrush, after cleaning the toilet with it."

The couple now look sick and worried; the man however breaks into the loudest laughter that I have ever heard, even the other passengers look over to see what the joke is.

"Go on honey, tell us some more," he splutters, also in an American accent.

"Well, I could go on, but they are much along the same lines. Just don't upset the crew and you will be ok. Oh and never start an argument, because they will label you as an offensive passenger and get the Police to meet the aircraft and cart you off at the other end. You could get a day in court and appear on the 6-o'clock news, for upsetting the crew."

The couple now look worried, but the man is still laughing.

Ginge comes back and raises her eyebrows at me. She asks everyone if they want anything and the couple politely decline and head back to their seats, which sets the man off laughing again. Ginge looks at me and raises her eyes and says to the man,

"Oh, I see my friend has been up to her old tricks again."

He carries on laughing and says,

"Pleased to meet you, young lady, my name is

Edward, but you can call me Teddy, most of my friends do."

"Then I am very pleased to be counted as one of your friends Teddy, my name is Maddie and this is Ginge, we're flatmates."

This is nice, I now have two people to talk to, this should kill some more time.

"What are you going to New York for?" Teddy asks us.

"Well, Ginge is off to her boyfriend's sister's wedding and is going to be meeting his family for the first time. I am here to support her, as he is embarrassed by his family and is worried that if Ginge meets them, she won't like him anymore. We have a feeling that they might be Trailer Trash."

This sets him off again. What a jolly time we're having.

Ginge gets called away again, and he says,

"How about you Maddie, don't you have anyone to look after you in New York?"

"Yes, Teddy as a matter of fact I do, but he doesn't know I'm coming yet and he may be really annoyed if I show up."

"Why on earth would he be annoyed about you coming?" Teddy looks incredulously at me.

"Oh, it's a long story that I won't bore you about. He is here on business and doesn't like to mix business with pleasure."

Ginge comes back and asks if we fancy a cup of tea or coffee. That sounds nice so I order a tea and Teddy a coffee. She hands over a plate of biscuits, she knows me so well.

"Would you like a biscuit Teddy, they are really nice."

"Thanks, he says taking one and says,

"Anyway, tell me the long story; I am certainly not going anywhere."

"Well, funnily enough, it has to do with Biscuits." He raises his eyebrows in surprise and I continue.

"James, my boyfriend, is in New York, to pitch for an advertising contract, to represent an American biscuit company in Europe."

Teddy looks interested, so I continue.

"Well, quite honestly I think he is on a ticket to nowhere with his advert and have told him so. However, he tells me that his bitch of an assistant, Ava, has some insider knowledge and has told him that it is exactly what the company are looking for and they would definitely be chosen over the competition."

Teddy looks surprised. "So why won't he listen to you when you told him that his Ad sucks."

"Because Ava has brainwashed him. I mean he is very clever normally and for some reason, she has made him believe that this is the way to win the contract. I personally don't trust her as I think she is devious. I don't know what her game is, but at least Jeremy is there to keep an eye on her."

Teddy looks like he is having trouble keeping up.

"Who's Jeremy, her boyfriend?"

I laugh saying, "Oh no Jeremy has a boyfriend of his own. he is James's PA and a good friend to me. He hates Ava too and also believes that she is up to something."

Teddy sits there obviously taking it all in.

Gosh, these biscuits are gorgeous, I offer Teddy some more.

"You know what Teddy; I think that whoever this biscuit God is, is probably the luckiest guy in the world."

Teddy almost chokes on his biscuit and I try to remember the correct procedure for helping a choking victim.

"Why do you say that?" he stutters.

"Well, whoever makes biscuits is a God in my eyes. I mean everyone loves a biscuit, don't they? There are all sorts and they come in all shapes and sizes. There are different flavours and combinations. You can do a lot with a biscuit. They can be just something to dunk in your tea while watching TV. You can get them out and arrange them on a plate to impress your friends, who come over for tea and biscuits. They can be dressed up, or down, according to the occasion and they can be the cheapest thing you'll buy or quite expensive depending on the packaging."

"You seem to know a lot about biscuits young lady, I have never seen anyone so passionate about a biscuit in my life."

"Well, I spend a lot of time thinking about them. If you think about it, there aren't many foods that have the versatility of a biscuit."

Teddy laughs again and says,

"Well enlighten me then."

"Well Teddy, a biscuit can be eaten at any time of the day. You can eat it in bed in the morning with a cup of tea and then again as a mid-morning snack. In fact, the only time you don't is when you are having dinner, but then you can eat one for dessert, as there are many uses for a biscuit in the dessert world. I always carry an emergency pack of biscuits in my car in case I am stranded in traffic and need food. Their shelf life is good, although they never last a week in my flat."

Teddy is obviously enjoying my biscuit rant because he looks very interested.

"In fact, Teddy, I even have an emergency pack in my hand luggage. The trouble is I cannot take them into America in case they harbour some form of European germs. I would be happy to share them with you."

"I would love that; it interests me to see what you

consider an emergency biscuit." He obviously finds the thought amusing as he chuckles.

"Well definitely not chocolate because they could melt. A good hard ginger nut is usually a good option."

I jump down to retrieve the packet. When I get back Teddy is looking thoughtful.

"Well Maddie, given your passion about the biscuit world, I am surprised that your boyfriend didn't take you up on some of your ideas."

"I've told you; I am the pleasure in his life, not the business. He can't appear to do both."

Ginge appears and says,

"Hi Maddie, I'm on my break now, do you want to come and have a chat?"

I am actually having fun talking to Teddy, but excuse myself and leaving him with a good supply of my biscuits I follow Ginge to the crew area.

She kicks off her cabin shoes; she changes from the stilettos into flats once the door closes, much more practical to walk to America in.

"Are you ok Maddie, not too bored?"

"On the contrary, I am having a great time. Now what is the plan when we get there?"

"Well, Tommy is sending a driver to pick us up and take us to his apartment. We are heading out for something to eat later and then the dreaded meeting first thing in the morning. Apparently, the wedding is in the Hamptons, so we will be heading off there later on in the day and staying overnight for the wedding in the morning."

"Don't you have to rush back after the wedding to catch the return flight?"

"Well, luckily, it's a four day stop, so we should be able to fit everything in. What are you going to do about James?"

"I thought that I would wait until after the meeting and surprise him. That way the business will be done so he can't accuse me of distracting him."

"When is it?"

"Tomorrow morning, so hopefully we will have a few days to have fun and may even be able to take in a show on Broadway and see the Statue of Liberty."

"Do you know where the meeting is?"

"Yes, Jeremy gave me the address; I told him that I needed it for emergency purposes."

Ginge laughs. "He must think you're mad?"

"Oh, he doesn't just think it, he knows it."

We then spend the next hour talking about the passengers and crew and what shops we must hit in New York. All too soon Ginge must go back to work and I head off to my Pod to watch another film and eat another meal.

John F Kennedy Airport - New York

We have now landed and retrieved our luggage. I saw Teddy in Customs and he came over to say goodbye.

"Well Maddie, it's been a pleasure meeting you and I must thank you for sharing your emergency biscuits with me."

"The pleasure was all mine Teddy."

He gives me his business card and says,

"If you need anything while you are here please give me a call. I could probably recommend a good biscuit if you want me to."

This sets him off laughing again - he is such a jolly sort.

I hand him mine saying, "Next time you are in the UK Teddy give me a call. Maybe we could meet up for elevenses?"

He looks down at my card which says,

Scentastic

Madison Brown

Territory Consultant

With my number on it.

"Consultant hey, are you as passionate about scented products as you are about biscuits?"

"Of course, Teddy, however, I am paid to be passionate about those, whereas the biscuits are more of a hobby obsession, really."

We shake hands and he heads through Customs and out into the hustle and bustle of the Airport.

As Ginge and I head through, we see a sign with our names on it being held aloft.

It says, "Ginny & Maddie."

We head over to it and the driver shows us to the waiting car.

Tommy's Apartment - 5th Avenue

Wow, Tommy has the coolest apartment. It is everything that I would imagine a Rock Star's home to be like. It is quite minimalist with lots of chrome and glass. There are fluffy rugs everywhere and various music memorabilia framed on the walls. These include his gold discs, guitars and posters for concerts. There are pictures in frames on the walls, that contain photos of Tommy meeting various celebrities. However, the biggest and most prominent is a canvas overhanging the settee which is a black-and-white photo of Ginge and Tommy laughing together, with their heads together. They look so happy and it is a beautiful image.

Tommy isn't here yet; apparently, he is still at the recording studio so Ginge and I decide to grab some sleep.

She shows me to the guest room which overlooks the Manhattan skyline. The room is huge and has a massive ensuite. She shows me Tommy's room, which is double the size and has a huge round bed with silk sheets and fluffy throws all over it. Gosh, a round bed, I wonder how comfortable that would really be. I would probably fall out. There are mirrors everywhere and the ensuite has a sunken bath and a double shower. The floor is marble with underfloor heating and there are large white fluffy towels folded up on the side.

We grab a drink and then decide to turn in. They are 5 hours behind us here so it is about 9 pm our time, but only 4 pm New York time. We are going out to eat at 7 pm, so have a couple of hours to sleep before getting ready.

6.30pm - New York Time

Ginge shakes me awake and says,

"Wake up Maddie, it's time to get ready and get something to eat."

For a minute, I think that we're at home in the flat, but then I realise that we are in New York.

It is with great excitement that I get ready and then head off to find Ginge and Tommy sitting curled up on the settee together.

Tommy jumps up and gives me an unexpected hug.

"Hi Maddie, good to see you again. Welcome to my home. Treat it like yours all the time you are here."

Gosh, he is very welcoming. He pulls Ginge up and lifts her high in the air.

Laughing and squealing she says, "Put me down Tommy, you'll embarrass Maddie."

He pulls her towards him and they don't come up for air for quite a while. I stand there not sure what to do. I don't know where to look really and feel a bit like an intruder.

Breaking away they laugh and Tommy says,

"Sorry Maddie, I can't keep my hands off this little one. We spend far too much time apart for my liking, so have to make up for it when we see each other."

Ginge is grinning and I say,

"Oh, don't worry about me, just carry on and pretend I'm not here."

Tommy grins and says lasciviously, "We had better not do that, I don't want to shock you on your first trip here."

Ginge pretends to hit him, but her eyes are full of love.

"Come on girls, I have two dates tonight for dinner, good for my image."

We follow him downstairs and out to the waiting car.

8.00pm - The Cosmopolitan Bar

Tommy has booked us a table at a great place to eat. Apparently, it is really difficult to get a table, but it is never a problem if you are as famous as he is.

It has a real buzz about it and we have been given a discreet table away from the prying eyes of the other diners.

It doesn't stop people from walking past and staring at him though. He seems oblivious and only has eyes for Ginge, but I notice them and think how strange it must be to be in the public eye.

The conversation turns to the next couple of days and Tommy instantly stiffens up looking worried. Ginge looks reassuringly at him and once again I wonder what can be so bad about his family. Maybe they are villains. He is part Italian so they could be the Mafia, wanted on several continents for drug trafficking and murder! I revised my original opinion about trailer trash when I found out that they lived in the Hamptons.

We have a great meal, but given the time difference, I am starting to flag. Tommy doesn't want to hang around either as he is keen to get Ginge back to the apartment; they can't even keep their hands off each other during dinner! I wish James was here. All this sexual tension is rubbing off on me. I wonder what he is doing now?

May 6th - 7am Local Time

I can't sleep any longer because of the time difference. It's about 12 pm at home and I never sleep in that late.

I get ready and head out to the kitchen. It is quiet; Tommy and Ginge must still be in bed. I know they are meeting Tommy's parents for morning coffee, so probably won't sleep in late, but I don't want to disturb them so decide to head off outside and get a coffee somewhere. Tommy gave me a key last night so that I could come and go as I please. I quickly scribble them a note and make my way to the lift.

Once I am on the ground floor I say, "Good day," to the doorman and go through the revolving doors on to the sidewalk.

It's already very busy and I decide to turn right and look for a deli or café. Maybe I can grab some breakfast for everyone?

I love London, but I decide that I also love New York. The yellow taxis speed past the wide streets and little jets of steam litter the pavements from the subway below. There are people on the corners selling newspapers and confectionery, just like at home and huge billboards advertise everything from consumables, to TV programmes.

There are lots of people jogging which puts me to shame. I can't even jog to the post box, which is about 200 yards from our front door, without having to walk back with a stitch. Maybe I should have included getting fit in my New Year's Resolutions? Oh well, never mind all that, I feel like a nice Danish pastry for breakfast, with a full-fat Latte.

I spy a likely establishment across the street and decide to try to cross the road to reach it. This is easier said than done. The streets here are wider than at home and the traffic is driving on the wrong side of the road. As soon as I think it's clear, something else is coming from the other direction. After trying for about the longest five minutes of my life, I decide to walk the 100 yards to the crossing. I never bother at home and just dodge the traffic as it slows down for the traffic lights. Even the lights are different here and there is an illuminated hand that tells you when it is safe to cross. No Green Cross man here, just the finger!

The deli is just what I had hoped for. There are some little tables set out just outside the door and it appears to be quite popular as it is heaving even at this early hour. I patiently wait my turn and look at the big blackboards on the walls behind the counter, displaying the menu of what's on offer. I decide to get three Lattes and Danish pastries.

The server is an Italian looking woman with a broad New York accent. She hears the different accent as I order and says,

"Hey, you're not from these parts are you, where are you from? Oh, no don't tell me I am good with accents, is it Australia?"

"Good guess, but incorrect," I say smiling at her.

"I am from the UK."

"I knew it," she answers loudly which makes me smile; has she forgotten that she said Australia?

"I'm British you know," she says and I look at her in surprise.

"Yeah, my ancestors came from Italy, but one of them married an English woman. I think she was my great great, great, great, Grandmother."

"Great," I say,

"We could be related."

She chuckles to herself and replies, "Never say never. Hey Marco, this lady is from England. She may know your cousin Vinnie."

I look around and see her addressing a customer sitting at a table near the window.

He looks up and shouts back,

"Yeah, he lives in a place called Essex, do you know him? I think the shop he runs is called Vinnie's."

I say, "No I can't say that I know it, but I'll look out for it if I'm ever in Essex."

"There you go," says the server.

"It's a small world isn't it."

I pay her the money and chuckling to myself head back to Tommy's apartment. Learning from my mistake, I cross at the crossing and am soon back.

Ginge and Tommy are up and very grateful for the breakfast. I am not sure if Tommy has any food in this apartment. He probably eats out all the time. He could do with a Cardigan Darren next door.

They both seem quite tense due to the morning coffee date looming. Ginge says,

"Maddie, after our meeting Tommy has to go back to the studio for a couple of hours before we head off to the Hamptons. Would you like to go shopping? I must find a dress to wear for the wedding and Tommy says that you can come too if you want, so you may need something as well. He has given me his credit card so the trips on him."

Tommy smiles indulgently at her and adds,

"Yeah, Maddie say you'll come, it will be good for Ginny to have a friend there."

Oh, this is awkward. I really wanted to track James down and now they want me to go to a stranger's wedding. However, I do owe them that at least. I mean they are paying for everything, it's the least I can do, really. Ginge then remembers James and adds,

"What time does James's meeting finish? Do you think we have time to go shopping before you meet him?"

"I think it finishes at 3 pm, so I am sure that we do."

"Invite him to the wedding as well," says Tommy.

"I will send a car to pick you both up from here tomorrow at about 9 am if that's ok?"

"Ok, thanks," I say hoping that I do get to see James. I might well miss him at this rate. I haven't let him know that I'm here yet because I want to surprise him. I thought that I would get a cab to the address that Jeremy gave me. I know it finishes at about 3 pm because they don't start there until about 2 pm, after lunch. I am not sure how long the presentations will go on for, so hopefully, I will have loads of time.

Ginge and Tommy get ready and with gloomy faces head off to meet his parents.

They say that they will only be about an hour and a half so I decide to spend the morning watching American television, splayed out on the couch.

12pm

Ginge is back alone. Tommy has gone to the studio, and she is looking very sombre.

I can't wait to hear how it went. We make ourselves a coffee and sit down for a chat.

"Come on Ginge, I can't wait to hear what they're like. Are they Mafioso?"

She shakes her head sadly and says sorrowfully,

"It's worse than we thought."

Goodness, I am surprised. They must be really bad because Ginge can always see the good in everyone.

She puts her head in her hands and looks despairingly at me.

"Poor Tommy, no wonder he's embarrassed. If his fans knew he would lose all credibility."

"Oh, for goodness' sake Ginge just tell me." I almost shout at her, this is so annoying.

"Well, it would have been better for Tommy if they were trailer trash, at least he could hold his head up with pride. The fact is Maddie, Tommy's parents; well his father anyway, is a Politician!"

Well, I wasn't expecting this. The shock must be registered all over my face. She carries on.

"His father is a Senator for the United States Government and his mother is one of those politicians' wives that are the powerhouse behind the man. Apparently, they had high hopes for Tommy to follow his father down the political path and were so disappointed that he became an International Rock Star instead. They kept on calling him Thomas, which I could tell was really winding him up and when they asked me what, Ginny, was short for and I told them they kept on calling me Virginia after that. His mother, Jennifer is her name, almost died and went to heaven when she found out that I had a double-barrelled surname and kept on going on about how British my accent was."

She slumps back in the seat and says sadly,

"If anyone was put off anyone, it was probably Tommy being put off me, the way his mother was fawning all over me."

"Never, Tommy loves you. He knows what his parents are like; after all, he did warn you about them. So how was it left?"

"Well, we have to go to the wedding as planned. They kept on going on about Tommy wearing a suit and being an usher, but he was having none of it. He told them that they were lucky he was coming at all and to make sure that there were seats at his table for two more guests, otherwise, he wouldn't be staying."

Gosh, that would be me and James. He still doesn't know any of this; I wonder what he will make of it.

"Anyway, we had better get going as we need to find some killer outfits for the wedding."

1pm - Saks Fifth Avenue

We are having the time of our life trying on loads of outfits in the womenswear department at Saks, which is only just down the street from Tommy's apartment.

We don't just stop at dresses, we try on shoes, accessories and look at handbags.

I feel guilty at the thought of Tommy footing the bill, but Ginge says that he won't mind. Whatever we spend won't even register with him, so we may as well have fun.

Ginge, as always looks fabulous in everything she tries on, but settles for a pale blue silky dress, Grecian style, with matching leather shoes and handbag.

I go for an emerald green silk dress, also with matching shoes and handbag. I try not to look at the total when it is rung through, but can't help but see it. $3000!!

I feel quite ill, but Ginge laughs at me and says that the last time she went shopping with Tommy's card, she spent $5000 and he didn't bat an eyelid.

Why is it that I am the only one that thinks it obscene to spend so much money on frivolities? I would have enjoyed it much more if we had gone to a bargain store and got everything we wanted for $100. I would have been beside myself with excitement at that. I hate paying full price for anything because I know that it will be on sale in no time at all and then I would get more for my money.

2.30pm

Ginge suddenly looks at her watch and says worriedly, "Maddie, you need to go. By the time, you find a cab and get to the meeting it will be past 3 pm. I can take these back to the apartment for you. Will you be alright though? I hate leaving you on your own in a strange city."

"Don't worry Ginge, I'll be fine. You go and I'll see you tomorrow at the wedding. Wish me luck with James."

She hugs me and says, "Good luck Maddie, I'll look forward to hearing all about it tomorrow. I wish that I wasn't going to this wedding, we could have had so much fun the four of us instead."

I wave goodbye and rush out onto the sidewalk. There are yellow taxis everywhere but none appear to want to stop. Maybe if I throw myself in front of one that would do the trick. I read once that you must be aggressive in hailing taxis here.

With my new remembered knowledge, I hold my hand up in a more forceful manner and with surprise see one drawing to a stop next to me. Gosh, who would have thought, the power of positive thinking?

Actually, it was only stopping to let someone out, but I took my chance and dived straight in.

"Where to Doll?" The cab driver says. I hand him the slip of paper with the address on that Jeremy had given me.

"Hold on then Doll, I'll get you there in no time."

Where are the seat belts? When he said hold on, I didn't think that I would need to take it literally. Do they even have driving tests over here? It's like being on the Waltzer at the fairground. I hope it isn't far; I may need to throw up in a minute.

Thankfully it only takes 15 minutes, and he squeals to a stop. My legs are really shaking and I struggle to get out of the car. I hand him the money and a tip - you must tip in America it's in the constitution- and look in front of me at the tall building that is home to, Bellini Biscuits.

Bellini Biscuits

I look up at the huge Skyscraper before me. I have to crane my neck to see to the top and I cannot imagine how many floors there are here.

There are many people coming and going and looking like they have a purpose. I think of James somewhere inside hopefully making his dreams come true. Once he has an American client the sky's the limit - or in this case the Skyscraper.

I walk towards the entrance, still not sure if this is the right thing to do. What if he is really annoyed? Oh well, I'm here now, I may as well get it over with.

Once inside, I find myself in a huge lobby. There is a desk in front of me and what looks like copious amounts of elevators, transporting the workers and visitors upwards. It is quite crowded with people going about their daily business.

My fear of lifts is coming back to haunt me, so I think I will just wait down here for it to finish. The receptionist is looking at me so I go over and say,

"Oh hi, is this the right place for the Bellini Biscuit advertising presentation?"

The receptionist smiles at me and checks her computer screen.

"Yes, it's on level 35 in the New Jersey suite. If you would like to sign in first, I will get you a visitor's badge."

"Oh, that's ok; I am just waiting for somebody who is inside. Can I wait at the reception for him?"

"Yes, that will be fine, but you will still need to sign in I'm afraid."

I take up the pen and sign my name and she hands me a visitor's badge in a plastic holder.

"You can take a seat over there, Miss Brown; hopefully, they shouldn't be much longer."

I smile at her and take a seat as requested.

I feel nervous for James and picture him here signing in as I have just done, just a short time before me. The trouble is, I can also picture Ava next to him. I hope she managed to pack a smile; she could freeze the sun with her poker face.

I daren't pick up a nearby magazine in case I miss him leaving, so I just look towards the lifts trying to spot a familiar face.

I must have sat here for about ten minutes when suddenly I do spot a familiar face and a very unexpected one at that. The lift has just opened and I see Teddy striding towards me.

"Maddie, what a pleasant surprise," he says beaming at me.

"Teddy, fancy seeing you here. Is this where you work?"

"Well yes, it is, what a coincidence."

"Yes, isn't it?" I say grinning at him.

"I am here to wait for James, he doesn't know I'm here yet, it's a big surprise."

"Oh, yes the presentation, well why don't you come up with me and we'll surprise him."

I shake my head in alarm.

"I couldn't, he may in the middle of things and I don't want to distract him. It's better if I just wait here."

"Nonsense, we can slip in at the back, he won't even know you're there."

My curiosity is getting the better of me and I decide that it would be more fun to see what's going on. Trouble is I must negotiate the elevator first.

As we wait, I ask Teddy, "Do you know where it is, I mean will they let us in?"

He laughs again and says,

"Yes, I think we will be alright."

Then a terrible thought strikes me and I look at him nervously.

"Teddy, you aren't bidding for this contract yourself, are you?"

Once again, he laughs heartily; I mean it's not that funny.

"No, I am just observing. It's been very interesting though. There have been some good ideas and some rather terrible ones too."

I wince thinking of Biscog, hoping that he is not referring to him.

The lift arrives and we step inside. Three more people follow us in and we press the button for the 35th floor. We stand there silently; is it my imagination or are the other people looking nervous too? They keep on glancing sideways at us and then quickly looking away. Maybe they have a phobia about lifts too. I am beginning to think that life in New York must be very stressful.

In no time at all, we reach level 35 and I am grateful to get out. The others look relieved that we have left, how strange!

I follow Teddy down the corridor to a large door at the end. As he opens it, I can see that the room is full of people all facing towards a stage, where there is a microphone set up and a big sign on the wall behind saying, Bellini Biscuits.

Teddy gestures to two seats at the back and we sit down to watch.

I look around but can see no sign of James, Jeremy or Ava. The man on the stage appears to be finishing his presentation, as the only thing I hear him say is, "And so the Biscith has landed." WHAT?!!!

I look at Teddy and raise my eyes, what on earth was that all about; maybe Biscog has a chance after all.

Teddy laughs again at my expression and appears to be enjoying himself.

Then I see her. Sitting a few rows in front of me, I just catch a glimpse of the harsh profile that is unmistakably Ava. Her face looks devoid of any expression, or emotion. I quickly look to see if James is next to her, and I am staggered to see not James, or Jeremy, but Beardy man!

I do a double take, is it really Rosemary his wife? I am dying to get a closer look and shift around in my chair to see. Gosh, any minute now and the chair will tip up. Teddy is looking at me wondering why I am so fidgety, so I say in a whisper.

"I can see Ava, but she is not with James, she appears to be with his rival. I knew it, I told James that she was up to no good, but he didn't listen."

I point her out to Teddy and he looks at them with a frown. I scan the room anxiously and then my heart flips over as I spy James, sitting in the second row from the front, with Jeremy next to him.

He looks so gorgeous and I want to run right up to him and jump on him. I've missed him so much.

Teddy is watching me with interest and I whisper again,

"Look there's James, 2nd row, wearing the smart navy suit and pink tie. His assistant Jeremy is next to him. Isn't he gorgeous?"

Teddy smiles and says, "He looks a great guy who I

might add is also a very lucky one. There are not many girlfriends who would take as much trouble as you have to surprise them."

I grin.

"He's very special that's why."

Teddy looks deep in thought and then a woman comes onto the stage.

"Well thank you RT&Co, that has given us lots to think about and wraps up our presentations. We would like to thank you all for coming and for all the hard work that you have obviously put in over the last few months. As you know, Bellini Biscuits wants to take Europe by storm and we are looking for a partner to work with, who believes totally in the concept and has our best interests at heart. The decision will soon be made and we thank you for your patience during this lengthy process.

Now before you leave, I would like to invite our Chairman and owner of Bellini Biscuits to the stage to close the session. Ladies and Gentlemen, I would like to introduce you to, Edward Standon.

DOUBLE WHAT?!!!

I look incredulously at Teddy, who winks at me and whispers,

"Listen, Maddie; just remember that whatever happens next you must trust me. Promise me?"

I nod in bewilderment and he heads off up to the stage. This can't be right. Teddy, the God of

Biscuits. I slump back into my seat trying to take it all in.

Teddy strides up onto the stage and stands before the gathering. He looks around at everyone and says,

"I would like to echo the words of, Barbara and thank you all for your presentations. You have obviously put in a large amount of work over several months and I do appreciate it. As you know, Bellini Biscuits is a very successful brand in the United States and I can see it doing as well in Europe with the right people behind it. It is time for us to branch out overseas and develop our business quite considerably."

He pauses and I look at him still trying to take it all in. I am trying to think what I said to him and hope that I haven't dropped James in it in any way. Teddy continues speaking.

"I have just returned from London after having viewed some potential distribution centres. I believe that I have found a satisfactory one, so if all goes well, we could be looking at launching the campaign in September."

There is a general buzz of conversation at this news, as it means that the contract would need to be awarded sooner, rather than later.

He carries on.

"However, as it happens, I had a very interesting flight back here yesterday."

Oh No! This doesn't sound good. I start squirming on my seat wondering what is coming next.

"I met a very interesting young woman who certainly gave me food for thought. I have never met anyone who is as passionate about biscuits as even me. She was totally unaware that I had any connection at all with a biscuit brand and we had a very interesting chat about the product and its many uses."

He is now looking over at me and I can feel my face burning.

"Ladies and Gentlemen, I would love to introduce you to my new friend, who as it happens could be with us today. Come up here Maddie and say hi to everyone."

Please let the ground open and swallow me whole! This is now my worst nightmare. How on earth could Teddy think this is a good thing?

It appears that the whole room is now looking for the mystery lady and so I have no choice. My face burning, I stand up and staring straight ahead of me, make my way to the stage. I absolutely cannot look in James's direction. He is going to be so mad; this is his worst nightmare coming true. The worlds of business and pleasure colliding with devastating consequences.

Teddy holds out his hands and I join him on stage feeling very awkward indeed. Teddy then carries on.

"Maddie gave me more to think about in 10 minutes of conversation than anything I have seen or heard over the last few months. It got me thinking and made me realise that what we need is somebody who is passionate about the brand. Somebody who understands it and is, in fact, one of its potential customers. Maddie is that person in my eyes and she is the only person that I want to handle my account in Europe."

WHAT?! Doesn't he remember that I sell home fragrance? I know nothing at all about advertising and launching a brand. I could probably sell it, but the rest is alien to me. I look at him in confusion and he smiles a reassuring smile at me.

"I am aware that this is not her field and so would need the back up of an established agency. Therefore, whoever employs this young lady, will win the contract. It is now up to you to persuade her that you are the best option for her career. If, however, she is unable to accept this change of direction, then I would have to revert back to the original plan and choose the next best thing."

I think I need to sit down. My life has changed in the last 5 minutes and I can't take it all in. I look for James and see him staring at me with disbelief written all over his face. I will him to give me some sign of reassurance, all I want is for him to charge up here and take over and reassure me that everything will be alright.

He appears to be frozen to the spot just staring at

me. Jeremy is also looking stunned. This isn't fair; this wasn't what was supposed to happen today.

Suddenly there is a crowd of people heading up to me thrusting me their business cards and asking me lots of questions. I can't see James now and I am starting to panic.

Beardy man appears before me and tries to grab my arm to steer me away from the crowd. Ava is looking daggers at me - nothing new there - and there appears to be a mad sense of chaos in the room.

Teddy holds his hands up and says, "Ok everyone, back to your seats."

The crowd disperses, but when I look, James and Jeremy appear to have gone. Anxiously I scan the room but they are nowhere to be seen.

Teddy wraps it all up by saying,

"Please leave me your cards and I will pass them on to Maddie. She will call each one of you, in turn, to find out your proposals. Now I am afraid that we have another meeting to attend so Barbara will sort everything out this end and you can direct your questions to her. Come on Maddie, let's go."

Numbly I follow Teddy out of the room.

Teddy's Office

I am sitting in Teddy's office trying to understand what has just happened. Teddy has asked his assistant to make me a cup of tea for the shock.

He is sitting opposite me looking at me with concern.

"Why Teddy? Whatever was that all about?" I say looking at him hoping for some kind of explanation.

"Maddie, since I first met you and our conversation developed, I felt a great connection with you. You say it how it is and I like that quality in a person. I know that you could do this job standing on your head, it is all there, you just need direction. I haven't built up my business without taking a few calculated risks and I am usually right in the end. Trust me, you can do this and if your boyfriend is half the man you say he is, he will find a way to work it out."

My eyes fill with tears at the mention of James. He must really hate me now. The look on his face will haunt me forever. He left without even speaking to me and I am scared that he will never want to see me again. I only wanted to surprise and support him and now I have undone everything that we have in 5 minutes.

"What do I do now Teddy?" I ask him, hoping that

he will fix it all for me.

"Finish your tea and I will get you a cab back to your friend's apartment. Sleep on it and wait and see what happens. I will be in touch with any offers that we receive, but somehow I very much doubt that you will be needing them."

Teddy accompanies me down in the lift. He says,

"Listen, Maddie, it will all work out, trust me. I really want to work with you. I think you are a brilliant person with some fantastic ideas and will go far in life. This is a good opportunity for you to progress and make a good career for yourself. Just sleep on it and don't make any rash decisions."

"What like you, Teddy?" I say smiling weakly at him. He laughs and says,

"This wasn't a rash decision; I have thought of nothing else since our conversation. I have had this planned and knew that you would turn up here today. I asked my receptionist to keep an eye out for you and as soon as you signed in, she was on the phone informing me of your arrival. So, you see, so far so good."

I have to laugh, am I really that predictable?

Soon we are in the vast reception area and I shake Teddy's hand.

"Thank you, Teddy, for believing in me. I will be in touch."

As I turn to leave, I suddenly see Jeremy sitting in

the reception. He sees me and comes racing over.

"Oh, my God Maddie, I can't believe what just happened. When did you get here and what on earth is going on?"

Frantically I look around to see if James is with him.

"Please Jeremy, where is James? I need to speak to him. Is he really mad at me?"

Jeremy's face is grim, and he says,

"James asked me to wait for you. He said that he would be waiting for you at the coffee house over the road."

He walked with me outside and pointed to a coffee shop on the corner of the street.

"Good Luck Maddie," he says.

I look at him in alarm and say,

"Oh, aren't you coming?"

He shakes his head,

"No, I am going back to the hotel. Let me know how it goes though."

I must look worried because he hugs me and says,

"Don't worry, you will be ok. James loves you; you'll work it out, I know it."

I wish I could be so confident I thought, scared of what might happen in the next half an hour.

The Coffee House

I cross the street and find myself standing in front of the brown and white façade of a trendy-looking coffee shop. I think to myself that my fate is about to be determined over a full-fat Latte.

I push the door open and look around for James. Suddenly I see him near the back in a booth and with trepidation, I approach him.

He looks up and I notice that his expression is still one of total shock.

I don't know what to do and just shift from one foot to another not sure whether I should sit down, or carry on standing.

All at once he jumps up and grabs hold of me almost squeezing the life out of me.

Oh No, maybe he is the coffee house slayer, and he is going to murder me!

It all gets too much for me and I break down sobbing in his arms.

He strokes my hair and says, "There, there, Maddie, don't cry I can't bear it."

I feel so relieved to be in his arms, that I don't want him to stop holding me. The events of the last hour have now well and truly caught up with me and I think that shock has set in.

He pulls away and dries my tears with his fingers, kissing me so passionately, that I am taken aback by its ferocity.

I am very confused. He pulls me next to him in the booth and holds me against him.

"Don't cry Maddie, I can't believe that you are here. I have missed you so much and when I saw you standing there looking at me, I just wanted to run up and hold you and never let you go."

I look at him, now extremely confused.

"But I thought that you would be angry with me. I have crossed the line between business and pleasure. I didn't mean to though, I only wanted to surprise you. I didn't know that Teddy was the owner of, Bellini Biscuits. We were only having a laugh on the plane."

James suddenly starts laughing and despite my confusion I join in.

"Maddie, you always manage to surprise me, that is what I love about you. Only you could walk in and land a contract that everyone else has been working on for months on end, by merely just having a laugh."

Just then the waitress comes over and James orders me a Latte. "Are you hungry would you like to eat anything?"

"I could do with a muffin if there's one going."

"Two muffins as well please, whatever you would

recommend."

The waitress looks at us and says, "Gee are you guys Australian?"

Oh, not this again. James smiles and says,

"No, we're from England, actually."

"Oh, I'm from England too," she says happily,

For goodness' sake, is this a standard response over here?

I look at James and we both burst out laughing. Thank goodness, the relief is overwhelming.

We sit there just holding hands, glad to be together again. James suddenly looks serious and says,

"You have quite a decision to make, don't you?"

I look at him and frown. "Please, James tell me what you think I should do? I mean I love my job at Scentastic, but this is a huge opportunity and they don't come my way very often. The trouble is, I know nothing about advertising and launching a brand."

He is looking very thoughtful and then says,

"You underestimate your ability, Maddie. Mr Standon is right, you are a natural for this and I am sure that your ideas would be far better than most of the ones pitched in that room. It is a subject close to your heart and I am sure that you would be very good at it. There is probably not an agency there that isn't now extremely desperate to sign you up, and you could probably name your price."

I look at him fearful of the answer to my next question.

"And does that include JS Public Relations and Marketing?"

He frowns and I feel him tense beside me.

"I'm not sure Maddie. I'm not saying I don't think you would be a huge asset to my business, in fact I know you would. The trouble is, I don't want you to be one of my employees. I love you and don't want anything to come before that. Let me think about it. I am sure that we will find a way. When do you have to let Mr Standon know your decision?"

Despondently I say, "He told me to sleep on it and he would forward anything from the other companies onto me."

"Good, then we have some time."

Suddenly, I remember Ava and say,

"James, what happened with Ava? I saw her sitting with that man you introduced me to at the charity auction, who also happens to be the one I thought I saw her with that day in London."

James flushes and suddenly looks very angry.

"Maddie, I owe you a huge apology on that one. As you know, we have built this campaign around Ava's supposed insider knowledge, which despite my misgivings and, may I add, yours and Jeremy's, we decided to run with. Well, on the morning of the presentation, we all met in reception. Ava then decides to inform us that she has received another job offer with Quentin's company and was handing in her notice effective immediately."

I always knew she was a bitch! Poor James. I squeeze his hand sympathetically and he carries on.

"I remembered what you had told me and asked her if they had been meeting up before this trip and if she had divulged any information about the campaign. She denied that she had, but I am not that obtuse and realised that you must have been right all along. Jeremy didn't pull his punches though and told her, in no uncertain terms, that she was a bitch who had obviously planned this and that you had been right not to trust her."

I laugh to myself, good old Jeremy.

"Well she just smiled at him, an evil sort of smile and left and we never saw her again. That is until she pitched up with Quentin at the presentation."

"I'm so sorry James; I thought that I'd got it wrong when I saw his wife. Maybe they are sisters and this has been their plan all along, to sabotage your pitch and make you look inadequate. Although, if she is his sister-in-law, I hope that it wasn't her I saw him with by the river, it was quite gross watching them all over each other."

James laughs and some of the tension leaves his face.

"Jeremy thinks that you were right and they must have been having an affair. He says that people always go for the same type and just because she is the image of his wife, it doesn't mean they are related. She could be his mistress."

"Typical Jeremy, although he has probably hit the nail on the head this time."

"What was their presentation like? Out of interest."

"I am sorry to say it was actually very good. I would have gone with them over everyone there. They certainly knew how to get ahead of the competition and I feel so stupid for not trusting my instincts."

"Don't worry James; I'm sure Teddy knows that they have been underhanded."

I smile and James looks at me with an unfathomable expression on his face.

"Anyway Maddie, enough about all of this, I want to know how you came to be here at all and where you are staying."

"Oh yes, I came with Ginge who is on a trip to meet Tommy's family and go to his sister's wedding, which we have been invited to, incidentally. I am staying at his apartment in 5th Avenue, which is amazing I might add. We go home in two days' time."

James laughs and says, "Well my flight is also in two days' time, so I suggest we make the most of the rest of our time here and what I want most of all is to spend it with you, preferably in my hotel room."

I laugh feeling very happy, all my worries fading into the background, as we leave the coffee house.

"James, would you like to come back to Tommy's apartment? I would love to show you and we could stay there. He is sending a car to pick us up from there in the morning to go to the wedding. If you want to of course."

I suddenly feel unsure; I mean James might not want to go to a stranger's wedding.

"I would love to Maddie; we could stop by my hotel and pick up my stuff. I need to see Jeremy anyway."

"Oh, I forgot about Jeremy, we can't leave him out."

"Don't worry about him, Felipe has also flown out and they are visiting friends on Broadway. I was meant to be going to a show with them this evening, but after the last experience, I am not sure that I trust their judgement. I wasn't looking forward to it as it is described as- an alternative Thriller - whatever that is supposed to mean."

We hail a taxi and head off to James's hotel.

Tommy's Apartment

I filled James in on the meeting with Tommy's parents and he was as surprised as I was. He is up for going to the wedding though and thinks it might be quite interesting.

I'm not so sure.

When we get to the apartment, James is as blown away as I was. I mean it is seriously fabulous, who wouldn't want to live here?

I notice that Ginge has left me a note, asking me to call her when I get back so that she can check that I have returned safely. I dial the number and she soon answers.

"Maddie, thank God you're back safely. I was worried; I don't like to think of you on your own, running around a strange city. How did it go, did you find James?"

"Oh Ginge, you would never believe what happened, yes I did find him, but I will have to fill you in tomorrow, as it's quite a story."

"But you're ok though?"

"Yes, James is with me now. Is it ok if he stays the night here too?"

"Of course, it is. I'm just glad that you're not on your own."

"How are things there? Has Tommy calmed down yet?"

Ginge sighs and sounds worried.

"It's not been brilliant. Tommy is getting really wound up. His sister is lovely, and he says that the only reason we are here is because he loves her so much, although he is not so sure of the guy she is marrying. Apparently, he went to school with his brother and they didn't get on. They want him to go out with the men tonight. I've been invited along to his sister's drinks evening with her bridesmaids and the mothers."

"Oh, are you going?"

"Tommy has told them no way. He said that he doesn't spend enough time with me and he doesn't want to waste any of the time that we do have together, by going out with people he doesn't like. He's told them that we will have one drink with his sister; then we have other plans."

"Oh my, that's awkward for you."

She sighs wearily.

"Yes, it's very awkward as I don't want to upset anyone, but at the same time, I only want to be with him. I wish you and James were here."

"Don't worry, just get through tonight and we'll see you in the morning."

I put the phone down and James looks at me with concern.

"Is everything ok?"

"Well put it this way, Tommy would rather not be there and Ginge is having to act as a mediator. The sooner we get there to help her out the better."

James comes over and pulls me towards him and kisses me like he has never kissed me before.

"I have missed you so much, Maddie. These last few days have been tough, and they have made me realise just how much I need you with me."

Gosh and there I was thinking that he wouldn't be pleased to see me.

He grabs hold of me again and picks me up and carries me to the bedroom.

"Let's make the most of our evening, shall we?"

Maybe it's something in the ventilation system in this apartment; it appears to bring out the caveman in our boyfriends. Oh well, I'm not complaining.

May 7th Tommy's Sister's Wedding Day

Well, what a night we had. After spending most of it in bed, we decided to order takeout and ate it looking out over 5th Avenue. Neither of us wanted to go out as we had everything we wanted right here.

Luckily, James has his smartest suit with him and had also coincidentally packed an emerald green tie. We match perfectly.

As I emerge in my new outfit, he looks at me with a stunned expression.

"Maddie, you look beautiful. Your outfit is fabulous."

"Oh, this old thing," I say jokingly.

"Actually, I only bought it yesterday, Ginge, and I had a shopping spree with Tommy's credit card."

James doesn't look very pleased at this and now I am feeling guilty again.

"I'm not sure I like the idea of some other guy buying my girl things." He says petulantly.

"Oh, don't be silly James; I am sure we will be able to pay him back in some way."

James looks thoughtful, what is it with male pride?

9am

The car has arrived to pick us up and take us to the wedding. The driver is called Donny and is very talkative. We get a running commentary of all the places that we pass, it turns out he used to run city tours and can't break the habit.

The city soon fades away and we now find ourselves on the outskirts of town heading towards the coast. I love America. Everything seems exciting and different, just like in the films. It is so big in contrast to England, it's no wonder that they think that we know everybody there, they must think that our country is the size of New York.

Soon we are at the coast and the houses get grander and grander. I laugh to myself picturing Tommy's family as Trailer Trash. I couldn't have been further away from the truth.

12pm - Tommy's Parent's House - The Hamptons

We have arrived at Tommy's parent's house and it is absolutely amazing. The drive in alone is about a mile long and it obviously sits right by the water's edge, as we can see the beautiful sea sparkling behind it.

The house itself is impressive. It looks like an old colonial mansion, everything I would expect a successful American politician to own.

As we draw near to the front door, I see Ginge waiting outside for us, looking drop dead gorgeous as usual in her blue dress.

"Maddie, James, you made it!"

She shouts and rushes up to me and gives me a hug.

"Come on I'll show you where to go. Tommy is inside."

The entrance hall is like something out of, Gone with the Wind. I am so excited. An American wedding. I wonder if they are different from ours.

Ginge takes us through the house to the garden. We can see lots of tables and chairs have been set up, either side of a red carpet, that leads down to a rose covered gazebo by the water's edge. There are flowers everywhere and there is a string quartet playing nearby. Waiters and waitresses are carrying huge silver trays, laden down with what looks like Champagne.

Ginge grabs one of their attention and we all help ourselves.

There are lots and lots of people milling around, all looking splendid in their wedding finery.

I cling onto James's hand. I am not letting go of it for a minute. This place is so intimidating.

She leads us over to a huge tree, under which I can see Tommy standing talking to a young man. I smile to myself, as Tommy has decided to stay true to himself and is wearing a black suit with a white t-shirt and his signature Rock Star shades.

He sees us coming and smiles looking pleased to see us.

"Maddie, James, good to see you. Come and meet my little brother Austin."

"Pleased to meet you," I say to the young man who looks about 15 and is dressed in a smart blue suit, with a white shirt and pale pink tie.

He smiles shyly at us and I am surprised to see that he looks like a younger version of Tommy - albeit a smart one.

"Austin was just telling me that Mom is in full, Mother-of-the-Bride, mode inside. It's best to stay out of her way, otherwise, you will get roped into something."

He pulls Ginge next to him as though he can't bear to be without her for a second.

A very smart man walks towards us and instantly I see Tommy's expression change from relaxed, to full of tension.

"Thomas, introduce me to your friends."

Well, that was to the point. No pleasantries for this man.

Tommy says almost sulkily, "Dad meet Maddie and James, our friends from England."

He looks at us and I feel as though I am being

appraised. James squeezes my hand; he is obviously affected by this man too.

"Frank Johnson, Thomas's father," he barks, extending his hand towards James and then me. He almost squeezes the life out of my hand and I try not to wince.

"Good to meet you both. Now, Thomas, I need you to come and meet some people."

Tommy looks angrily at him, but decides to go, he probably can't say no. They head off but Ginge stays with us. Austin also follows them. Thankfully we are now alone.

"Well, Tommy isn't much like his Father." I say feeling quite shocked, actually.

Ginge looks worried.

"No, they are like chalk and cheese. Tommy hates all the goings on in the world of politics and tries to keep away from them. He hates the falseness of it and how corrupt they all are. His Father can't understand the entertainment business and has never even been to one of Tommy's concerts. Even though Tommy has made it big and made more money than even his parents, they still hope that he will come to his senses and join them in their world."

James looks shocked.

"Poor Tommy, no wonder he didn't want you to meet them," he says sympathetically.

Ginge carries on.

"They wanted him to meet a suitable American girl, who would back him in a political career like his mother does. They must hate it that his girlfriend is an Air Stewardess and not even American."

"They know nothing then," I say angrily. Ginge is the best thing that could ever happen to Tommy; luckily, he knows it.

"Why is Tommy called Carzola if his family name is Johnson?" I say suddenly remembering his surname.

Ginge smiles. "Carzola is his grandmother's maiden name. He absolutely adores her and it sounds much more rock-and-roll than Johnson. Also, he can distance himself from his family so that he is not associated with them."

Just then Tommy comes back and says,

"Come on guys, let's find a seat. They're gonna be starting soon. The sooner this is over the better."

We follow him to find a seat and he guides us all into a row at the back. The furthest away from his family I note with a smile.

The seats all fill up and I can't help noticing lots of interested looks thrown Tommy's way, as the guests file past. He, of course, is oblivious and is more interested in playing with Ginge's hair and giving her the odd kiss.

Suddenly, a patrician-looking woman stands at the end of the row and fixes him with a stern look.

"Thomas, why aren't you sitting near the front with the family? Your seat is there with us, not skulking at the back."

This must be his mother I note with interest. Tommy looks at her with a blank expression on his face.

"Sorry, Mom didn't think. I'll be fine here don't worry."

The music starts up signifying the arrival of the bride and his mother gives him a withering look and heads towards the front.

I look at James, who looks as uncomfortable as I feel and I raise my eyes. Ginge looks embarrassed, but Tommy just grabs her hand and gives her a wink.

I look around me with interest. The place is packed and there are even people standing. The weather is gorgeous, blue skies and sunshine. I wonder what would have happened if it had rained? We would probably have had to go indoors. That's the trouble with living in a rainy country, you always expect it to rain and it's just a bonus if it doesn't.

Then there is a buzz of excitement as the wedding party arrives. I haven't managed to sneak a look at the Groom yet, but as I turn around, I see the most gorgeous little flower girls walking along, throwing flower petals out of cute little wicker baskets. Little page boys follow them, looking like they would rather be anywhere else than here and who can blame them given the mini tuxedos they have been crammed into.

James looks at me and smiles. I do so love him. I am glad that I followed him out here. I know we still have a major hurdle to overcome, but none of that means anything compared to how I feel about him.

Then I see the bride walking sedately down the red carpet clinging on to her father, Senator Johnson. She is beautiful and her dress is amazing. Ginge nudges me and I see Tommy looking proudly at his sister. Well, at least he loves his brother and sister, even if his parents are a nightmare.

She sees Tommy and her eyes fill up with tears. I see her mouth the words, "Thank you", as she walks past. This has obviously been quite a sacrifice for Tommy to be here and I wonder just how deep this rift with his parents goes.

The service is beautiful. They have even written their own vows. I am totally going to write my own vows one day. They would be deep and soul searching and would probably be streamed on the web and adopted by other couples everywhere. They would be the "Viral vows" and would probably change the shape of weddings to come in the future. In fact, the whole experience is bringing a tear to my eye; weddings always have this effect on me. I could have a career as a professional guest as I cry at everything. The worst is funerals. There was this one time that I ended up at the wrong funeral. How was I to know that the people going in were the funeral before my Uncle Jim's? I know I got the time wrong, but there should be a law that they only have one a day in my opinion. Talk about a conveyor belt. By the end of it, I was in floods of tears for poor Ruby Mackintosh, she had lived such a colourful life and I will never forget her. The Vicar looked quite concerned for me as I staggered past him after the service.

James nudges me and guiltily I realise that I have drifted off as everyone is standing to sing. Shame I don't know the song, as I love to sing at the top of my voice at Church. I like to picture myself as that opera singer, Katherine Jenkins. With proper training, I think that I could give her a run for her money.

I crane my neck to see the Groom. He looks ok; I wonder what Tommy has against him. They are gazing into each other's eyes as they exchange rings. I look at Ginge to see if she has a tissue, oh for goodness' sake do they ever stop kissing these two? No wonder Tommy wanted to sit at the back. Cinemas I get but you would think that his sister's wedding would take priority. I look at James and raise my eyes in disbelief.

He grins at me and pulls me against him. Maybe weddings bring out the romance in everyone. Well, I'm not complaining.

Soon the service is over and the wedding party walk back down the aisle to claps and cheers. Ginge says,

"Thank goodness, now we can get a drink. I think I've got a suntan just standing here. I'm melting."

Yes, it is hot; I am beginning to regret buying a silk dress. Looking at Ginge, I marvel at how she still looks as cool as a cucumber - although why cucumbers are considered cool is anyone's guess - I have never seen her sweat in my life.

Tommy grabs hold of her hand and says to us all,

"Come on let's get out of here before we're roped in to any photographs."

He leads us over the manicured lawn towards his favourite shady tree and we hide behind it away from the gathering crowd.

We must have only sat here for about 10 minutes before Tommy's brother finds us.

"Tommy, Mom's going mad over there. Morgan wants a photo with you and Ginny."

With a sigh, Tommy stands up and pulls Ginge up with him.

"Come on baby let's get this over with. James, Maddie why don't you get a drink and we'll come and find you."

We all troop over towards the crowd and Tommy and Ginge disappear off, over to where the happy couple is posing for photographs.

"Let's get a drink," James says and we accost a

passing waitress and take two glasses of Champagne from her tray.

"That was a lovely service." James says unexpectedly. I wouldn't have had him down as the sentimental type. I nod in agreement.

"It's interesting looking at the guests, isn't it? I mean, they all look really well to do and there are all sorts here. Tommy looks totally out of place among this lot."

James laughs in agreement.

We stand here people watching for a good half an hour and then Ginge finds us and says that we are all moving into the marquee for food.

"We'll have to join the queue for the lineup," she says,

"I've lost Tommy but we may as well just go in. I know where we are sitting."

Oh, no a line-up. I never know what to say to people I know at these things, let alone people I know nothing about. Ginge laughs at my expression.

"Just say, you look lovely to the ladies and well done to the men. That's what I always say. You're past in a flash and they are always looking at the next person, anyway."

We all laugh and follow her inside.

Well, that was interesting. It took about half an hour to reach the front of the line. I followed the script, and it wasn't so bad. Tommy's parents scare the hell out of me and I was a stuttering wreck when it came to my time. His sister Morgan was lovely; she hugged us all and thanked us for coming. She said she knew that Tommy wouldn't have come unless we were there to support him and so she was eternally grateful to us. Her husband was a bit of a creep, actually. He couldn't take his eyes off Ginge and held on to her hand for far too long. He also smiled at me in a creepy sort of way and I thought that she would probably have trouble ahead with him.

We found out that we were sitting on a table near to the top table with Tommy, his brother Austin and his grandmother, as well as a few more of Tommy's relations.

It all looks lovely. The colour scheme is pink and blue and there are ornate candelabras festooned with roses and cornflowers amongst which sit ivory candles. Each place setting has a small pink or blue box, depending on the gender of the recipient which contain a selection of Belgian Chocolates. There is wine on each of the tables and we all help ourselves to whichever we prefer.

I am sitting with James on one side and Ginge on the other. She is next to Tommy, of course, and he is next to his grandmother, with Austin next to her the other side. Apparently, his Aunt, Uncle and two cousins make up the ten of us.

Tommy's grandmother, or Nana, as he calls her is

hilarious, a real character. She has a definite twinkle in her eye and he obviously adores her. Nana looks as pleased as punch to be sitting between her two grandsons and keeps us entertained with tales of them as little boys.

She leans over and says to Ginge and me, "Tommy has restored my faith in my family. At last, I have someone to be proud of. His Grandfather would also have been so proud. Thank goodness, he didn't follow in my son's footsteps; it would have been too much to bear. Politicians in the family, shameful!"

We laugh, glad to hear that at least one member of his family is proud of him.

She says to Tommy, "Will you be playing me a song later? I do hope so, it's all I've been looking forward to."

Tommy looks worried; Ginge tells me,

"He doesn't want to perform; he says that if his family can't be bothered to come and see him in one of his concerts, why should he put himself out for them here."

Good point.

Luckily, he is spared from answering as the waiters come around with the starters.

We are served, Terrine of Foie Gras, with Blackcurrant Jelly and Summer Berries.

I'm not so sure of Foie Gras, so gave mine to

James, who in turn gave me his Summer Berries. It's great having someone to swap food with. Nana was most upset as she was hoping for Melon Balls.

Looking around, I notice several people keep on staring over at Tommy and Ginge. They are obviously the subject of much scrutiny, him being the black sheep of the family, as well as being super famous. Ginge is just beauty personified and always attracts attention. They, in turn, don't even notice, as they are too wrapped up in each other to even care.

The next course arrives which is, Fillet of Beef with a Burgundy Jus and mousseline potatoes. I'm quite glad I came now; the food is divine despite being the product of mass catering. The wine is good too and I am glad that we don't have to drive, what a wasted opportunity that would have been.

Tommy's Aunt and Uncle are also good company. He owns a car dealership, and she is a stay at home Mom, even though his two cousins left home two years ago. Oh well, maybe they visit a lot.

Dessert arrives in the form of, baked blueberry cheesecake with chocolate crumble and mascarpone sorbet. Gosh, Masterchef eat your heart out. I could get used to fine dining. James got none of that, in fact, I was rather hoping that he would give me his as well.

Soon it was time for the speeches, which I always look forward to at weddings, even if I don't know the people involved. I just love to watch the speech makers getting more and more worried as the meal goes on. I really hope for some embarrassing stories, preferably involving the Bridegroom on his stag night.

The speeches go quite well although are rather tiresome. They lack any real humour and are a bit boring, really. The Senator's speech is mainly an excuse to push his views on everyone and score political points. The guests appear to enjoy it though, probably because politics is all that anyone thinks of here it seems. Nana fell asleep between dessert and coffee so has thankfully been spared the boredom.

I look with interest at the Best Man, as he is Tommy's nemesis from school. He looks the preppy sort to me, the total opposite of Tommy, no wonder they didn't get along.

He does the usual trick of thanking the bridesmaids who giggle and flutter their eyelashes at him, maybe he is considered quite a catch and they are hoping the rumour is true that the Best Man always gets off with the Bridesmaid.

As soon as it's all finished Tommy grabs hold of Ginge and excuses them from the table.

"We won't be long, just got a few things to do before the evening reception," Tommy says and Ginge blushes. This time James raises his eyebrows at me, they just never stop!

We decide to go for a walk along the beach. It is a beautiful day and it will be nice to have some time alone. It has been quite a day already.

The beach is deserted, and the sun is beginning to set. This could be paradise. I am so happy that James is here with me and I am determined to put all thoughts of career-changing opportunities out of my mind.

James places his jacket on the sand and pulls me down next to him. We sit there cuddling looking at the sun dying down over the horizon, only to rise again somewhere else. I think it's quite symbolic really of my situation. The end of something that has run its course and the beginning of a new opportunity. I sink my head onto James's shoulder and try to just enjoy this moment with the man I love.

7.30pm - The Evening Bash

After our romantic moment on the beach James and I return just in time to see the evening guests arriving. There is to be a huge evening bash with about 200 hundred extra people descending on the Senator's house.

We make our way inside the marquee and head to the bar that has been set up for the evening. James orders us a gin and tonic each and we move to the side to watch the evening events unfold.

I see Ginge enter the marquee unusually on her own. I wave and she comes over.

"Hi Maddie, hi James, have you been alright? I'm sorry we left you."

Ginge has changed into another outfit. She looks like a real Rock Chick now, with a tight-fitting black crochet dress, with sharp black stilettos. Her hair is long and glowing golden in the light and she looks really hot.

"Where's Tommy?" I ask surprised that he is not at his usual place, super-glued to her side.

"Oh, he's got waylaid by his mother. She wanted to introduce him to some of her friends. He'll be along in a minute. Do you both need to freshen up? I can show you to our room if you like. Maddie, you can borrow something of mine if you want to change and I am sure that Tommy has something that you can borrow James."

In my dreams I think, Ginge is at least two sizes smaller than me and Tommy is probably two sizes bigger than James. I reply,

"Oh, don't worry, but it might be good to re-do my hair and makeup."

James says,

"Look, you two go, I'll be ok. I'll just find the gents and then I'll wait here."

"Ok I won't be long, I promise." I give James a kiss and head off with Ginge towards the house.

Tommy & Ginge's room

Tommy's childhood bedroom is quite a large room that has obviously been changed considerably since he must have occupied it. It is now lilac and very pretty. Not at all what I expected. Their clothes are everywhere and strewn all over the place. I try not to look at the unmade bed and am just glad that they are out of it for once.

I freshen up as Ginge tries to clear up, however, the perfect housewife she is not and I see her just kick it all under the bed.

"How are you bearing up?" I ask her, noticing how tired she suddenly looks.

"Oh, I'm fine. I hate this stage of our visits because all I can think of is that I have to go home tomorrow and won't see Tommy for a while again."

"How long this time?" I ask interested to see what Ginge considers a while. In my experience, the longest has been two weeks since they met a year ago, not bad for a long-distance relationship.

"Well I'm not seeing him until my trip to Los Angeles next Friday."

I laugh out loud,

"Ginge that will be exactly six days. It's hardly enough time to wash your clothes and re-pack your case. What on earth am I going to do with you? Stop worrying and just enjoy your evening."

Ginge laughs and says,

"You're right as usual. I suppose it's not so bad as we have a week there this time and I love spending time with Tommy at his house in LA. It's just the two of us, perfect."

As we make our way outside, we link arms together as we used to at school. She really is my best friend, always has been and always will. We are like best friends and sisters rolled into one. All at once we hear Tommy's name mentioned as we near the galleried landing. It is coming from beneath the stairs and we stop to listen.

"She's an Air Stewardess, I believe," we hear some female voice saying. We look at each other and carry on listening.

"Oh well that won't last, will it? I bet Tommy meets loads of girls every night, probably has one in every city he goes to, you know what these Rock Stars are like."

"Well I've heard they've been together for ages and he is really smitten."

The other voice laughs derisively.

"Well if you believe that you believe anything. My guess is as soon as she's on the plane home he's in bed with some groupie."

"Don't be such a cow Tiffany; you're just jealous because he dumped you some years back."

"Yes, well he'll come crawling back when he realises that he needs to find a proper woman and settle down. I mean when you think about it there's no real competition. His girlfriend lives in England and he lives in America. It's just a matter of time."

They move away and we can hear no more. Ginge looks at me and her face has turned white. She sinks down onto a nearby seat.

"Oh Maddie, is that really what people think? That it's a fling and can't go anywhere?"

I sit down beside her and put my arm around her.

"Don't be so silly, of course not. Tommy absolutely adores you; you know that. Who cares what some ex-girlfriend says anyway? She's just jealous it's obvious."

Ginge manages a weak smile.

"Yes, you're probably right. We had better get back, James was left on his own and Tommy will be wondering where I am."

However, as we walk back, I know that Ginge is thinking of nothing else but what we have just heard.

8.30pm

As we walk into the marquee, I can see James talking to Tommy where we had left him. Tommy has changed into more comfortable clothes, in keeping with his image. He is wearing faded jeans and a t-shirt that highlights his many tattoos. I notice Tommy look towards us and then frown as he sees us coming.

James smiles and then we hear the band starting; kicking off the evening entertainment.

"Come on, Maddie, let's dance," James says whisking me away. I notice Tommy and Ginge talking in the corner and whatever she says, he is still frowning.

I love dancing, I always have. Once I thought that I could be a professional dancer, but when I realised that you had to practice every day and do lots of boring routines, I gave it up and took up badminton instead. I prefer to freestyle.

After a while, we go back to our drinks for a break. Tommy and Ginge are still there, but I can sense that Ginge is not herself. Tommy's sister Morgan comes up and we all have a nice chat about the wedding and find out that she is off on Honeymoon to Paris. Oh, how romantic. I have never been unless you count the one-day school trip on the Eurotunnel to see the Eiffel Tower. Trips are so wasted on the young, all we wanted to do was eat our packed lunches and look at the hot French guys. Actually, I would still do that if I went now, some things never change.

Morgan asks Ginge if she could help her with her dress, as she needs the ladies, so Ginge dutifully goes off to help. Tommy turns to me and says,

"Maddie, what's up with Ginny? I know something is, but she says it's nothing."

"Oh, we just overheard some girls talking about you

both when we were inside."

He frowns and says,

"What did they say?"

"Well, they were just talking about the fact that your relationship probably wouldn't last and that you were likely to have a girl in every city when Ginge wasn't around. They also said you would get tired of her and find an American girl to settle down with."

Tommy's face is now like thunder and I wish that I hadn't told him.

"Do you know who said this?" he says in a low voice.

"I did remember the name but thought better of divulging it, so I shake my head.

James looks shocked and says, "Poor Ginge, that wasn't a nice conversation to hear."

Suddenly we hear a commotion by the door and there is lots of excited chatter reverberating around the marquee. We look towards the entrance and a smile breaks out over Tommy's face as he sees his band members making their big entrance.

He races over to greet them and I notice that suddenly every female in the place is in here and some of the men, lusting after their hot girlfriends.

I look over and see Tommy's mother looking resigned to the invasion and the place suddenly comes alive as the party is now well and truly underway.

10.30pm

I have never had so much fun at a wedding. I have danced and sang and drunk far too much wine. Ginge and I have re-visited our youth and partied the night away. Suddenly I notice a familiar face and do a double take.

"Look, James, isn't that Teddy?" I shout making myself heard over the loud music.

James looks over and nods, his face registering his surprise.

We rush over and Teddy looks delighted to see us.

"Maddie, how lovely to see you. This must be your boyfriend James, pleased to meet you."

James returns the greeting and I say,

"I didn't know you knew Tommy's family."

"What you mean the Trailer Trash?" Teddy says laughing loudly.

I blush, as James looks at me with a confused expression.

"Turns out I was wrong," I say sheepishly.

Teddy laughs loudly again, and we are joined by Senator and Mrs Johnson.

"Hi Frank," says Teddy.

"This is Maddie my English friend that I was telling you about and her boyfriend James, who is now also my friend by association."

Tommy's parents look surprised.

"Oh, that's a coincidence, they are also Thomas and Virginias friends, what a small world." the Senator says.

"Yes, I am hoping that Maddie will agree to help me take Europe by storm. I am just waiting for her decision."

The Senator looks surprised and says,

"Well young Lady, you shouldn't deliberate too long. Edward is a very astute businessman and if he sees potential in you, then you must be good."

They get called away and I note with satisfaction that he called Teddy, Edward. Hmm, not such a good friend after all. Teddy certainly is a good judge of character.

Ginge comes up and recognising Teddy says hi.

"Maddie let's dance," she says and pulls me away. As I look back, I notice James already deep in conversation with Teddy.

I can see Tommy dancing with his sister, so Ginge and I hit the floor with careless abandon. I am glad to see that she has cheered up.

11pm

We have just had the best evening buffet that I have ever seen at a wedding. The food earlier was sublime, and I thought that nothing else could top that, but this spread was amazing. There was a brilliant ice sculpture with all manner of fishy delights arranged around it, including lobster, oysters and mussels to name but a few. For the meat-eaters, there was all manner of cured meats and exotic salads and dips, with an array of artisan bread. We all grabbed loads and sat outside having an impromptu picnic.

Tommy's band are good company and I haven't laughed so much in ages.

Ginge and I decide to head inside the marquee, to grab some dessert and Tommy says,

"Ginge, grab a selection, I just need to borrow the guys for a minute, some wedding stuff I need to take care of. We won't be long."

I wonder what he can be up to. He is probably going to sabotage the going away car, or something. These wedding pranks are endless. It would be cool if they hid all their clothes and packed fancy dress costumes in their place. That I would love to see.

James goes off with them and I laugh to see him mingling with the Rockers. Actually, he doesn't look that out of place.

Ginge and I go inside and decide on what we should take. There are all sorts of delicious desserts and she picks up a huge bowl of profiteroles and strawberries.

"Maddie, you grab those little cake things over there and some serviettes. There should be enough here for everyone."

However, before we can even turn around, I am aware of somebody behind us. I spin around and see the groom's brother; I think his name is Brandon, standing closely behind Ginge. She also spins around and I notice that he looks extremely worse for wear.

"Well, Well," he says swaying around drunkenly.

"If it isn't the rock chick and her hot friend."

HOT! Maybe he's not that bad. Ok I know he's drunk.

"What are you wasting time on that loser Tommy for; you need to find yourself a real man."

Ginge looks worried and says, "Look I don't want any trouble, so just let us pass and we'll say nothing more about it."

He laughs and I look around to see if I can get any help, but the only people milling around don't seem to notice our difficulty and are too absorbed in their own evening to care.

"Trouble hey, well I kinda like trouble and you my dear have trouble written all over your lovely body."

He then presses his body against her, trapping her against the table.

"Stop that!" I shout.

"Get away from her; she is not interested in you. You're drunk, go and sleep it off somewhere."

I try to push in between them, but he shoves me and

I fall back against the table.

Why is nobody helping? I shout across at a lad attacking the chocolate cheesecake,

"Please, can you help us?"

He looks at Brandon and I see him visibly pale. He drops the cheesecake and runs out of the marquee. Huh, what a lot of help he was. I can't get help, as I won't leave Ginge. Meanwhile, she is shouting at him.

"Just leave me alone you're disgusting," and she tries to push him away, which appears to just make him more excited.

"Come on sweetheart, you know you want to, you rock chicks are all the same, begging for it."

Suddenly, all hell breaks loose. Tommy bursts into the marquee, closely followed by the band and James. With a howl of rage, he flies over and effortlessly drags Brandon away from Ginge who now looks utterly terrified. I see the man who ran out and realise that he went for help. Thank goodness.

Tommy lands a terrific punch on Brandon, who falls to the ground, blood spurting out of his nose.

"You stay away from my girlfriend you piece of shit," he shouts and Brandon, seeing everyone staring at him, jumps up saying, "You're welcome to her; you always had a thing for whores, anyway."

Well, that was obviously the wrong thing to say,

because Tommy just flew at him. Ginge is now crying, and it seems that the whole of the wedding is flooding in to see what the commotion is. We all watch in dismay, as Tommy and Brandon, are locked in a fight, totally destroying the buffet.

Tommy's band are obviously enjoying the spectacle and James races over to Ginge and I and grabs hold of us. Tommy's sister and her new husband rush in, closely followed by both sets of parents. They start shouting at Tommy to stop and then reluctantly the band step in and pull the two apart.

Tommy's mother gives him a withering stare and Brandon's family bundle him out of the marquee. His father looks angry but his sister suddenly starts laughing and says,

"That was a long time coming. Are you ok Tommy, Ginge?"

Tommy nods and grabs hold of Ginge, holding her close and saying, "It's ok baby, did he hurt you?"

She is still shaking and trying to stop the tears, obviously still in shock at the whole situation.

James holds me and says, "What about you, are you ok? Did he hurt you?"

"No, I'm fine," I say rubbing my wrist where he grabbed it and shoved me. He was certainly forceful.

The waiters and waitresses rush around, to start tidying up the mess and Tommy's mother says,

"I'll speak to you later Thomas. I had better go and apologise to Brandon and his parents for your behaviour. I suggest you start thinking about how you are going to apologise to them yourself."

His father added,

"You just couldn't hold it in, could you? You had to cause a scene at your sister's wedding and with her new brother-in-law. You are a disgrace."

And they left looking very angry.

Tommy looks angry and Ginge just puts her arms around him and holds him close.

"Thank you, Tommy, I do love you," she says.

He strokes her face tenderly and says,

"If he had hurt you, he wouldn't be walking out of here. You are the only thing that matters to me. I couldn't care less about the rest of them," and he gestured to the backs of his retreating parents.

"Come on," Tommy says suddenly grinning, let's grab what we can, we have our own party to go to."

12am - Midnight Beach party

I can't believe it. It turns out that Tommy and the rest weren't doing any wedding business at all, they were setting up a private beach party just for us. They have set up a little camp, with flaming torches and candles. There are huge blankets and throws dotted around and a campfire is burning in the middle. They have grabbed loads of drink and with the food that we managed to secure; it looks like the most romantic beach party that I have ever been to.

We all grab a spot and sit with our partners in a circle next to the ocean, that is bathed in moonlight.

The beach is deserted apart from us and I look at James thinking how lucky I am. He pulls me close and kisses me gently.

"I Love you, Maddie," he whispers, stroking my face gently.

"I love you more," I reply and kiss him again.

Suddenly the sky lights up with the fireworks from the wedding and we all settle down to watch them. They are truly spectacular and I feel as though we have the perfect spot in which to see them.

Tommy grabs his guitar that is propped up against a cooler and plays the most haunting love song that I have ever heard. Ginge is lying on her elbows, her hands propping up her chin, watching him with total adoration. The song is all about long-distance love and how it makes him feel. He must have written it for her and it brings a tear to my eye.

The rest of the band are relaxing with their girlfriends, totally chilling out after the drama that has just happened.

James wraps a blanket around us and we cuddle together on the sand, glad to be together, just enjoying the moment with all thoughts of what is to come firmly out of our minds.

May 8th Tommy's Apartment

James and I wake up in the spare room at Tommy's Apartment. We are exhausted after the marathon day yesterday.

After our little beach party, we left at around 3 am. Tommy and Ginge came with us, largely to escape the wrath of his parents. They just grabbed their stuff and left without even a goodbye. Tommy said that he would speak to his sister today and wish her luck, but he couldn't be bothered to face his parents.

Sadly, I remember that we have to leave today. The flight is at lunchtime and we must be at the airport by 12 pm. As it turns out James is also on the flight, so if Ginge manages to get me upgraded, I will be able to spend the return journey home with him.

We get ready and head out into the kitchen. Tommy and Ginge are still not up, so I decide to take James to my favourite café to get us some breakfast.

We are strolling along the sidewalk, once again mingling with the locals, busily on their way somewhere.

"I've had such a lovely time," I say to James, as we walk hand in hand along the street.

He nods and says,

"It seems like we have been here for ages. I can't believe that the presentation was only two days, ago can you?"

I shake my head, suddenly realisation setting in about the decision that I have to make."

Then I remember seeing James and Teddy chatting in deep conversation at the wedding and say,

"What were you talking to Teddy about at the wedding? You looked in deep conversation."

James smiles at me.

"Oh yes, I forgot to tell you what with all the excitement and everything."

"Tell me what?" I'm suddenly feeling apprehensive.

"Well Teddy thinks that he has a solution to our problem."

"Which is?" My mind is racing along at a hundred miles an hour. I am not sure that I can cope with life-changing solutions before my morning Latte.

We get to the café and James pushes the door open for me. The conversation stops as our breakfast order takes priority, but I am eaten up with curiosity. I can't believe that I have spent all evening and night with him and he is only just telling me now!

Out of interest, I look around for Marco, but he is nowhere to be seen, maybe he's in Essex visiting his cousin.

The server is the same lady though; she recognises

me probably because of my hair and offers up a cheery hi. 4x lattes and Danish pastries later - I am a creature of habit after all - we find ourselves walking back to the apartment.

"Well hurry up James, I'm dying to know what the solution is."

James laughs, obviously enjoying the fact that he is keeping it from me, which is obviously driving me mad.

"Well, Teddy thinks that rather than an agency employing you, it would be much better if he employed you directly as his voice, to work directly with the selected agency on the project."

What me? The voice of Bellini Biscuits. I picture my business card,

Madison Brown
Bellini Biscuits
The Voice.

Hmm doesn't have much of a ring to it.

"Sorry, James I don't understand?"

"Well, he needs to set up an office in Europe and he prefers the UK. He'll be appointing someone to run the operation there and will need to employ the relevant staff. Your job would be to liaise between the two organisations to come up with a strategy to launch the biscuits in Europe. He would like your ideas to be explored and you would have creative control over the project. The job would be ongoing, as he is also interested in your ideas on product development."

Gosh, this is unexpected and a lot to take in.

"Where are his offices going to be, Do you know? I mean I don't want to have to relocate you know."

"I'm not sure but I think that he was looking at the Kingston area."

Suddenly I am excited. Maybe I could do this. It's a bit scary but, she who dares wins after all. Then I have a not so pleasant thought.

"What if he awards the contract to Beardy man? I don't think I could work with Ava."

James laughs, but I fail to see what's funny about it.

"You won't have to because Teddy has awarded the contract to me."

I am stunned and look at him in confusion.

"Well, how will that work? You don't mix business and pleasure."

"Ordinarily, no I don't, however, I happen to think that we work well together and I wouldn't actually be employing you, if anything, it's the other way round and your word is final."

Wow, I feel the power flooding through me already. Madison Brown - The Voice!

Flight Home

Finally, we are on the way home. Luckily, I was upgraded as there was room in first class and James is in the Pod next to me. Jeremy decided to stay for the rest of the week with Felipe and their friends on Broadway.

Tommy is also on the flight. He was so incensed at the comments that we overheard, he decided that it's his turn to follow Ginge around the world and is coming to stay until they return to his home in LA next week. He booked himself a seat, as well as one for Mario. The thought of them all at the flat was worrying, but Tommy has booked them all into the Savoy Hotel in London, as a treat for Ginge.

I'm not looking forward to getting back to the daily grind, but know it's not going to be for long, as it looks like my new job is going to start next month. It is with much trepidation that I am going to have to compose my resignation letter.

Teddy phoned me at Tommy's apartment and confirmed what James had told me. The salary he is offering is about three times what I am on now, so I definitely couldn't turn it down.

We are all sitting at the Bar area on the flight. Tommy, as usual, is the focus of rather a lot of interest, but he is just watching Ginge go about her business and listening to his music. James and I are talking about the Biscuit project and I feel really important.

Ginge says, "I'm off for my break now, do you need anything before I go? I get about half an hour."

"Oh, we're fine," I say, feeling guilty that I haven't spent much time talking to her as she works.

"Do you want some company?"

"No thank you," she smiles blushing.

"Tommy's going to keep me company."

I look over and he is grinning suggestively. Looking at James, I raise my eyes in their direction and he laughs but doesn't look surprised.

Tommy and Ginge disappear off to the crew area, so James and I decide to go back to our pods and have a rest. The last few days have caught up with us a bit, so we decide to get some sleep.

Parkmead - Esher

Home at last. Tommy and Ginge went off to the Savoy and James went home.

It feels good to be back to normality, whatever that is and I decide to crash for the rest of the day. Cardigan Darren has left us some food, so I don't have to venture out and I am looking forward to some alone time.

Even though it's only been four days, it feels like four weeks. I am back to work for a few days and then, as promised, James and I are off to his house in Dorset for the weekend.

I am really looking forward to seeing It, as it's a large part of his life that I know nothing about. He has also invited Ginge and Tommy, to repay the favour from New York. He also mentioned asking the massage twins if they fancied it, as they are actually quite good company and he thought it would be fun to go as a group. Mind you, I have had enough group activity to last me a lifetime after the wedding, but at least I have a few days to recover.

James's House in Dorset

James picked me, Darren and Dessie up this morning and drove us to his house in Poole. Tommy, Ginge and Mario are coming later this evening. It is forecast to be a good weekend weather-wise, so James is hoping we can go out on his boat. Apparently, he has it moored at the end of his garden, which backs onto the harbour.

As we drive up to his house, I can feel his excitement building.

My first look at his house is breathtaking. It is a large modern house, with solar panels on the roof. He says that he had it designed to be eco-friendly and tried to make it as self-sufficient as possible. It has taken two years to complete and is very much his baby.

He drives into a large garage and we exit the car. He leads us through a door into the hallway. There is a large staircase in the middle and the house is filled with light, coming from the large windows and white walls. Even the floor is white marble and the light fittings are chrome.

He leads us through into the sitting room that has bi-fold doors leading onto a large deck area.

The house is huge and James proudly shows us around. He has installed the latest gadgets and technology and has once again used the services of an Interior designer, who has done a fantastic job. She has made it feel homely, yet practical, the perfect retreat.

The kitchen is massive and houses the obligatory coffee machine and built-in wine cooler. However, best of all is the master bedroom. It too has bi-fold doors, that lead out onto a private balcony, that houses a hot tub. The room itself is huge and there is a large king-sized bed facing out over the water.

The ensuite is home to a double walk-in shower and the largest bath that I have ever seen. There are, 'his and hers,' sinks and masses of large white fluffy towels and designer oils and lotions.

Darren and Dessie are as blown away as I am and James is clearly excited showing us around.

He shows them to one of the guest rooms, that is also very impressive, once again with its own private balcony and ensuite. It even has a little sitting area with a comfy settee, TV and tea and coffee making facilities, in case his guests want some space.

We leave them to settle in and James takes me back to his bedroom to unpack.

However, being around Tommy so much has obviously rubbed off on him, because it is some time before we think of unpacking.

We shower and change into something more comfortable and head outside to the decking area and sort out some drinks for our guests around the large comfortable seating outside.

Darren and Dessie soon materialise and we sit outside relaxing in the sunshine.

8pm

Tommy and Ginge arrived about an hour ago and were as blown away by the house as the rest of us. They also had a similar guest room and we decide to order a takeaway and just enjoy each other's company. Mario is also staying in the fourth bedroom but insists on keeping out of our way. He spends his evening watching TV and eating in his room. Tommy says he likes it that way. He is a good bodyguard but likes his own company. The trouble with having Tommy to stay is that we can't really venture out much, as he gets mobbed wherever he goes. It is just easier to stay in, although he does want to go out on the boat tomorrow.

We all turn in early, as we want an early start in the morning. At least that's our excuse!

Boat Trip

James has packed the boat up and we are all ready to embark - or whatever it is that you do when you get on a boat. James's pride and joy is called, Oscar and is a 65ft Sunseeker. I have to admit I am not very nautical, but even I am excited by it.

It's like an apartment on the sea and has everything, including bedrooms, bathroom, living room and kitchen. There is a sunbathing deck, or three and it is really cool.

"James, why did you call it Oscar?" Dessie asks him.

"Oscar was my dog as a child and I adored him." James says smiling at her.

"He used to follow me everywhere, and I was devastated when he died."

This brought tears to my eyes, imagining James and his childhood friend, inseparable until death.

James looks at me with concern.

"Maddie, are you crying?" he says astonished. Quickly I wipe my eyes and say,

"Oh, don't be so silly, I think I got some salt in my eye or something."

Ginge grins at me - she knows me so well.

We busy ourselves getting everything ready. James, Tommy and Darren do all the boaty things and us girls see to getting the drinks and nibbles ready.

Soon we are on our way and sailing the seven seas, or in this case, pottering around Poole Harbour.

James asks us if we fancy going over to Brownsea Island. Gosh, it makes us sound like the Famous Five, or in our case six. Although actually only one of us is famous. Maybe we'll have an adventure! The trouble is, we cannot get near it as it is too shallow, so we decide to go out of the harbour to a nearby Bay.

I have decided that I like boating. We are not sailing because there are no sails involved, just engines. The feel of the wind in my hair and watching the ocean spray really gives me a sense of freedom and I can totally see what James loves about it.

We soon moor off the Bay, which has a lovely golden sandy beach. It's too cold to go swimming, so we decide to just bob around drinking and eating. It's very relaxing and I can imagine it would be the perfect way to spend a summer's day.

James sits next to me; pulls me towards him and kisses me.

"Thank you for coming here, it means the world to me to have everything I love in the one place."

"Oh, I'm one of your things, now am I?" I say jokingly.

He grins and says, "The best thing I have ever had and may I add my most favourite."

I snuggle up next to him, as the boat gently rocks.

Everyone is really chilled and we have a lovely time just relaxing and recharging our batteries.

We head back after three hours and decide to go into the harbour for dinner this evening.

We walk to a nearby restaurant that James booked earlier. The food is meant to be good and after our boating experience, we are all ravenous.

The restaurant is dimly lit and we have a table for six in the corner.

The food and wine is good and soon we are full up and slightly drunk.

"What are your plans for the next few weeks, Ginge? I have sort of lost track."

"Well, we are going to LA on Tuesday for a week and then Tommy's European leg of the tour kicks off, so it will be back to commuting for a couple of months. How about you?"

"Well, I am going to hand in my resignation on Monday, which still makes me nervous. I'm due to start at Bellini Biscuits after that and Teddy wants me to go to New York for training."

Tommy says, "You can stay at my apartment if you like? It would be good to have someone there to keep an eye on it, as I don't get there much."

Gosh, living there for a week, how lucky am I?

"Thanks, Tommy, are you sure? I mean, I don't want to put you out."

He just smiles and winks at me. "Maybe James can meet you out there and you could make a trip of it?"

James looks disappointed. "I would have loved to, but because I have been away and spent so much time on the Biscuit bid, I have sort of neglected my other campaigns. I'm going to be really busy for the next few months."

Bother! This isn't good. I hate it when James is busy and with Ginge away most of the time, life is going to be very boring.

"What about you Darren?" Ginge says.

"Have you and Dessie got any plans?"

Darren looks excited and holding Dessie's hand says,

"Well actually, we are going to start a business together."

Wow, that is news. We all listen excitedly.

"We are going to set up a massage business, starting small in our spare time and hopefully it will do well and we can give up our day jobs. I'm going to study sports massage and then hopefully we will get recommended for Sport's injuries."

Dessie smiles saying,

"We can't wait. It's all very exciting and I can still do my hairdressing in the meantime."

We are very fortunate that Dessie is a qualified hairdresser and beautician. She has been doing mine and Ginge's hair for a month now and she is very good. It's also convenient as we don't even have to leave the flat and she can do it while we watch our favourite programmes.

We order our coffees and then Tommy is approached by a couple at the next table for a photograph. He obliges with good spirit and they are really grateful. I keep on forgetting that he is recognised wherever he goes, even in Dorset it would seem.

They decide to call Mario to come and get them, but James and I decide that we will walk back as it is a lovely evening. Darren and Dessie decide to share their lift and soon we find ourselves on our own walking back arm in arm along the harbour.

James seems in a reflective mood so I say,

"Is everything alright James? You seem quite quiet."

He squeezes my hand and says,

"I'm just sad that I will be so busy for the next few months. I would have liked to support you in your new job a bit more, but know what my workload is like and I worry that we won't spend so much time together."

I fight back the disappointment and smile at him saying,

"It won't be that long. I will be busy anyway learning a new job and things will settle down."

Suddenly he stops and holds me close. "I love you so much Maddie and can't bear to be away from you even for a night. It is going to be so hard for me."

He kisses me and holds me tightly against him.

"Well, there's always Skype," I say, not really

convincing myself it's a good substitution.

He laughs. "I know how Tommy must feel now. No wonder he writes Ginge so many songs, it's his way of keeping the connection. All I can do is design an Ad around you."

We laugh at the thought, but then I say,

"Never mind, we still have the Biscuit campaign and I have a feeling that I am going to need a lot of personal attention on that one."

We reach the house and once inside realise that everyone has already turned in for the night.

"Come on," James says.

"There's a hot tub to try out, let's make the most of the time that we do have."

I really love this house!!

July 6th - Bellini Biscuits

I am back in New York ready for my first day as The Voice of Bellini Biscuits, Europe. I flew in yesterday and spent the night at Tommy's apartment. It feels like home already and I even went back to my local café for the usual latte and Danish for my breakfast.

I got a cab to the office and am now sitting in Teddy's office for a catch-up.

My old company Scentastic were devastated that I left and tried to talk me out of leaving. The hardest person to tell was Matty who was my close friend there and I will really miss our chats and textathons. He said that if I ever needed a sales rep, then he would join us like a shot. Well, you never know?

Betty was quite matter of fact about it all, no love lost there anyway, but Brian was upset as we got along really well.

They all had a whip round and bought me John Lewis vouchers. It came to £200 so I'm going on a spree there when I get back. I got to keep all my samples, so the flat smells fantastic. I also gave some to Cardigan Darren. His flat does smell a bit better now that Dessie lives there, but old habits die hard and we still smell the odd pungent odour seeping through the ventilation system.

It is good to see Teddy again, and I was surprised to learn that he's feared amongst his employees. That would explain the nervous lift goers. I can't understand why, but then I haven't started working here yet, so that may all change.

"Maddie, I'm so glad you accepted my offer." He says, a broad smile on his face.

"You're going to be great and I can't wait to see the results."

I feel quite nervous now; I actually don't know where to start.

He presses a buzzer on his desk and asks his receptionist to send someone called Marie in and I look at him questioningly.

A woman comes into the room who I guess to be in her late forties. She is smartly dressed and has a severe blonde bob. She smiles warmly at me and introduces herself.

"I'm pleased to meet you," I say liking her immediately.

She sits down and Teddy says, "Marie is going to head up my organisation in Europe. She is moving over to London and will oversee the business there. You will work together to establish the brand. Maddie, you are in charge of product development and advertising and Marie will be in charge of logistics and running the warehousing and distribution. I'm sure you will work well together and both report back to me."

Marie smiles and says, "I'm looking forward to the challenge and working with you, Maddie. Please ask me anything, no matter how small it may seem. Don't worry about anything other than launching the brand; I'll take care of the rest."

Well, that's taken a load off my shoulders. She carries on.

"I'm leaving for London tomorrow to start the recruiting process and the fitting out of the warehouse. I will see you next Monday at the office in Kingston and we can get started."

Teddy then says, "Now I'll show you both around and then we can go out to lunch. Maddie, you will spend the week in the various departments, learning how things work here, a sort of induction process."

I nod excitedly and then we are off.

Tommy's Apartment - 8pm

I have just got back and am exhausted. Lunch was nice, and we all got along really well. Marie liked some of my ideas and Teddy kept us entertained with stories about the business.

I decide to Skype James, as I have missed him so much. He answers straight away and the sight of him makes my heart flip.

"Hi," he says softly; smiling that gorgeous smile of his.

"Hi," I say also smiling.

"How was it baby, I've been thinking of you all day?"

Why does he still make my heart beat faster? Even after all these months.

"It was great. Teddy is still the same fun Teddy that I remember and he introduced me to Marie, who is going to be running the operation in the UK. I feel a bit out on a limb though, you know, *The New Girl*."

He laughs.

"You're bound to feel like that at first. It will get better when you start properly and get into the swing of it."

"How are things there? Are you still really busy?"

"Yes, it's totally mad here. I will probably get away about 10 pm tonight as there is so much to do. Although, as you're away, I'm trying to do as much as possible so that I can spend all weekend with you."

How did I ever get so lucky to find him?

"I can't wait James; I really mean that. It's strange being here in Tommy's apartment without you and all I really want is to come home."

"Well, you'll be home in no time. Oh, I nearly forgot, my Mum and Dad are home in a couple of weeks and want us to meet up. They are really looking forward to meeting you and I thought that we could go to Dorset and do it then."

"Is that your birthday weekend?"

He smiles and raises his eyes. "Yes, but I don't want a fuss, just a meal out with them will be fine."

I grin at him, "Not even a cake?"

"Oh well, if you insist, but no candles."

I hear James's phone ringing and he groans, "Sorry, Maddie got to go, there's a conference call coming through. I love you and take care out there."

"I love you more. I'll call you tomorrow."

Then he is gone and I feel more alone than I did before. This business travel is not all it's cracked up to be.

July 10th - Parkmead Flat

Finally, I'm home. This week although exciting has dragged. I loved being in New York and spending time learning about my new company, but I missed James and home.

Ginge is also home and I haven't seen her in ages. Because of the flight and time difference, James said that he would come and pick me up in the morning so that I could sleep off the jet lag. I would rather sleep it off with him.

Oh well, a night in with Ginge is no hardship and we decide to slob around in our pyjamas and watch endless reality TV programmes that we have recorded. We have a good supply of chocolate so all is well.

I have filled her in on my new job and she, in turn, has filled me in on her week with Tommy. She is away again tomorrow for three days and is then flying to Paris where the Band are in concert. I would love to go there. It must be so romantic. In fact, I don't know why we don't just hop on the Euro tunnel and go one weekend. I think I'll suggest it to James. I would quite like a mini break.

Just then there is a knock on the door. I look at Ginge and say,

"Are you expecting anyone?"

"No, who do you think it can be?"

"Well, there's only one way to find out."

I open the door and see Dessie standing there looking really agitated.

"Dessie come in, what's the matter?"

Ginge looks at me with concern and I guide her over to the settee.

"I'm so mad with Darren. Do you think that I could cool off here for a bit?"

"Of course," Ginge says, "why what's he done?"

"He's being a total idiot that's what. I mean it's not my fault that his favourite cardigan got tangled up with my jumper and turned pink in the wash is it? Mistakes do happen and I didn't do it on purpose. He's just lucky that I do his washing at all."

I try not to smile and daren't look at Ginge.

"Oh, don't worry it's not that big a deal, he'll get over it," I say reassuringly.

She carries on ranting.

"I didn't say anything when he used up all my body lotion and it was my favourite. I also turned a blind eye when he cut his nails in the living room and they fell on the carpet."

AARGH GROSS!!!

Ginge looks sympathetic.

"That's the trouble with men they just don't think. Tommy can't even manage to re-stock his fridge.

We are always running out of food and drink, even the basics like white wine."

I laugh, thanking God that we at least have Cardigan Darren next door; otherwise we would also run out on a regular basis. Ginge is no domestic goddess and probably doesn't even know where the nearest supermarket is, anyway.

Dessie sniffs, looking a little calmer. "What about James?" Ginge says,

"I bet he has some annoying habits too?"

"Yes, he does actually," I say thinking about it,

"He is so OCD; everything has its place and has to be the right way around. I put a tin of tomatoes in his cupboard once and saw his expression when the label was facing the back. He pretended to go into it for something and I saw him turn the tin round to face the right way."

They laugh and Dessie says,

"Yes, Darren likes his food in order of freshness like at the supermarket. The newest have to go to the back and he gets really mad if I just put things away and buck the system."

"Well, James has this really annoying habit of turning the TV over when I am watching something. He only seems interested in programmes on cars and gadgets. He won't even watch, Made in Chelsea, and he has a house there. You would think that he would want to keep an eye on the neighbourhood wouldn't you?"

"Tommy only wants to watch programmes on the Discovery Channel and MTV. Although he gets really annoyed if he is on it and switches off. He is not at all interested in my programmes and says they are rubbish."

We all nod in agreement. "Why do men only like boring factual programmes? It's much more fun to see how other people live. I didn't know a thing about Essex until I started watching TOWIE." Dessie says looking puzzled.

This is so much fun. I love having a good moan about the opposite sex. They are great for many things but are a strange species, really.

I add, "James doesn't even like shopping. He orders whatever he needs online and can't see the point of it."

The others shake their heads in agreement.

Dessie says, "Darren just shadows me around the shop and if I ask if he likes anything he says - yes but do you need it - what's need got to do with shopping?"

Ginge says, "Just leave him in the cardigan section and that will buy you some peace and quiet. Tommy doesn't come shopping with me, but there was this one time he did and he just sat there on a chair messing around with his phone looking bored. It was only when I tried something sexy on that I got his attention. I had to insist that he couldn't follow me into the changing room. I never asked him after that and he just gives me his credit card."

Dessie says, "Do either of them have any annoying hobbies? Darren is into bird watching. He spends hours with his binoculars and a little notebook by the window box. He is always trying to tempt the birds to our window with various titbits. The trouble is it's me that has to clean the mess off the window. Do you know that he subscribes to a texting service where other like-minded people text if they spot something unusual? Last weekend he jumped out of bed and drove to Suffolk because there was a sighting of a lesser spotted something or another. He didn't get back until 7 pm and said that he missed it! At least I had the flat to myself and could watch back to back, Keeping up with the Kardashians."

We laugh at the thought of Darren's wasted journey.

Dessie then says to Ginge.

"Does Tommy have any embarrassing hobbies?"

Ginge suddenly looks uncomfortable and blushes. Oh, this is going to be good. I can't wait to hear what it is. I bet it's something really depraved judging by her expression.

"Oh, I'm not sure if I should tell you, I mean he wouldn't want it getting out."

Dessie and I exchange excited looks.

"Come on Ginge," I say. "We're all friends here, spill the beans."

Once again, she blushes and says,

"Well Tommy's hobby is more about something that he collects; he's more of a collector than a doer."

"What on earth is it? I can't wait." I almost scream at her.

She laughs. "Ok but don't tell him I told you, Tommy collects, Action Men."

Dessie and I look at each other puzzled. Is that it, no depraved sexual fetish or weird pastime?

"What, like the little doll figures with gripping hands and eagle eyes?" Dessie says looking confused.

This sets us all off, and it is some time before we compose ourselves.

Ginge wipes her eyes. "Yes, he has quite a collection at his house in LA. They are all in pristine condition and still in their boxes and some are worth thousands. He has dealers tracking them down around the world, who call him with any rare finds."

Once again, we can't stop laughing. Wiping my eyes, I say,

"And do you get your Barbie's out and play together?"

This sets Dessie off and Ginge throws cushions at

us.

I decide to grab the wine; this is turning into a fab evening.

As we all sit there Ginge suddenly says, "Do you remember when we first moved in and met Darren?"

I laugh. "How could I forget, it was hilarious? He knocked on the door to introduce himself and he was wearing his Starsky cardigan. We pretended that Ginge was Polish and didn't speak any English and he believed us."

Dessie laughs and Ginge carries on the tale.

"We kept it going for about three weeks, which was fine because I was away a lot, anyway. What we didn't know was that Darren had decided that he should learn some Polish in case of emergencies."

"That sounds like Darren," says Dessie grinning,

"I got home from a flight and before I could get inside Darren popped out of his flat and said something to me in Polish. I didn't know what he was talking about, but apparently, he said - 'Hi are you tired after your day at work?' - well, I had to confess to him right there and then."

Dessie looks interested.

"Was he cross at you?"

I say, "Yes for ages but he got his revenge."

Ginge laughs. "Oh yes, I remember. He helped Maddie's Dad out one day when he came over to decorate our living room. Well, Maddie's dad had to leave to pick up her Mum, so Darren said that he would finish off. When he had gone, he hung the last piece of wallpaper upside down."

Dessie looks shocked and we laugh fondly at the memory.

I point to the wall. "There it is, still there in the corner. The floor lamp is against it, but we call it, Revenge Corner. Such happy days."

"In fact, come to think of it, Darren really is such a great guy," I say smiling.

"He has put up with a lot from us and is always there if we need him. I wouldn't want to live next door to anyone else, really; I know I can rely on him."

Ginge nods her head in agreement and Dessie suddenly looks thoughtful and her eyes mist over.

"You know what, you're right, he is lovely; a bit strange, but then aren't we all?"

We nod in agreement. A knock at the door interrupts our thoughts and we all look at each other and grin.

I say, "Well no prizes for guessing who that is. The only question is what kind of chocolate is he is bearing?"

Dessie runs over and answers the door. Darren is standing there looking extremely worried and holding a giant bar of Galaxy. Before he can even speak she launches herself at him and squeezes the life out of him.

"Oh Darren, why are we arguing? I love you, you strange little man," and then she rains kisses all over his face.

Ginge and I look at each other and smile.

July 31ˢᵗ - The day before James's Birthday

Life has been so busy lately that I haven't even had time to think. Work is going well and I am really enjoying working with Marie. She is such fun and as there is so much to do, we are just getting on with it all as best as we can.

I have had a few meetings with James and Jeremy about the Biscuit campaign, which is progressing nicely. We have decided on the theme and James is bringing it all to life.

I have to admit he is very good at his job. It's no wonder he is so successful and sought after. It makes me even more surprised that he was sucked in by Ava. Luckily, we haven't crossed her path ever since, but I know it's just a matter of time.

I love working with him and Jeremy. We spend hours in his office after the close of business discussing ideas and looking at ways to make it even better. I then get to go to dinner with James and then back to his flat. We are settling into a cosy routine and I wish it could last forever.

This evening I am at home in Esher packing for the weekend. It's James's birthday tomorrow and we are going to Dorset later on tonight when James has finished work and picks me up. I'm looking forward to spending the weekend with him and meeting his parents, who he obviously loves to bits, so they can't be that bad.

It was difficult deciding on a present for him but I managed to get a photo put on a canvas of us at Tommy's sister's wedding, when we were sitting on the beach watching the sun go down.

I knew the selfie stick would come in handy one day.

I have also bought him a rare bottle of wine, as he collects wine and has quite a collection of it at his house in Dorset.

The doorbell rings and feeling excited I open it to see James lounging in the doorway looking gorgeous as usual. He smiles at me in the way that sets my heart racing and I fling myself at him unashamedly.

"That's a nice welcome," he says grinning at me as we come up for air.

"I've missed you that's all," I say meaning it.

"But we only went out for dinner two days ago," he says laughing.

"Are you saying that I can't miss my boyfriend if I want to?" I say with mock indignation. He grabs hold of me again and we decide to postpone our journey for a little while, while we catch up with each other in my bedroom.

James's Birthday - Dorset

We arrived late last night and just fell into bed exhausted.

We wake up at about 10 am and the weather is glorious. While James is in the shower, I put his presents on the bed and wait for him to come in.

He comes into the room wearing just a towel around his waist and notices the gift-wrapped packages and cards on the bed.

"Happy birthday baby", I say and pat the bed for him to sit down.

He looks at me excitedly and opens the gifts that I have laid out for him. As well as mine there are various gifts from my parents, Ginge, Tommy, Darren and Dessie.

Ginge and Tommy managed to get him a replica of his boat, which even had the name Oscar engraved on it.

"This is so cool," he says, his eyes lighting up.

"I am going to keep this in my office to remind me of my pride and joy."

Darren and Dessie have bought him an experience, in the form of a day out driving a racing car at Silverstone. He is such a speed freak, so it's perfect for him.

Mum and Dad have bought him some Champagne and tickets to Mamma Mia. He looks at me with raised eyebrows and I laugh saying,

"Well, they did ask for suggestions."

He looks at me and laughs and then pushes the gifts off the bed saying,

"I've saved the best present until last. It's the one I want most of all."

"But James aren't we meeting your parents?" I say suddenly anxious. What if they turn up and we are otherwise indisposed? I would be so embarrassed. James laughs pulling me closer.

"Not for two hours yet, that gives us one hour and fifty minutes to entertain ourselves."

I sigh with relief and relax just happy to be with the man I love.

12pm - Poole Harbour

We are meeting James's parents at a restaurant in Poole Harbour for lunch. I am so nervous. James said that there was no need as I would get along really well with them. I hope they are not like Tommy's.

They are already there and all I see is his Mum rushing over to give him a hug shouting, "Happy Birthday," at the top of her voice. Then she sees me and to my surprise envelops me in a big hug too.

"You must be Maddie; I'm so pleased to finally

meet you. James has told us lots about you, all good I might add and I have been so looking forward to putting a face to the name."

I smile shyly and say hello.

She stands there just looking at us and grinning and then his Dad comes over and also hugs James, wishing him a happy birthday. He doesn't hug me, but gives me a huge grin and kisses me on both cheeks.

"Maddie, I'm Terry and this whirlwind is Margaret. We are so pleased to meet you."

Gosh, I wasn't expecting them to be so open and friendly. I can see why James is so fabulous, his parents are too it seems.

James is grinning, obviously pleased to see them both.

"Come on our table is over here, you must be starving," Margaret says gesturing towards a table by the window overlooking the harbour.

I turn red thinking of the events of the last hour and realise just what an appetite I have worked up.

James laughs as he sees my face and grabs my hand and leads me to the table.

Margaret asks me many questions about myself and Terry wants to hear all about James's business. I find out they have a flat nearby overlooking the harbour.

Margaret says, "We sold our house to buy the flat

so we could go travelling. We like to go on Cruises and have just returned from the Caribbean. Have you ever been there Maddie?"

I shake my head and she carries on.

"We look after James's house here when we are home."

"Which is virtually never," interrupts Terry laughing.

They are so lucky, what a great life they are having. I look at James who is so obviously enjoying being with them and think of how hard he works. I wish that he could have more time off to enjoy his money, but he is so driven.

We enjoy our meal; they have so many interesting stories to tell of their travels, which makes my life seem really dull.

Terry insists on paying the bill and then James says,

"Would you like to come back for a coffee? I could take you out for a ride in Oscar if you want?"

Terry nods happily. It's obvious he would love to spend time with James, but Margaret shakes her head.

"You boys do that if you wish, but I wanted to ask Maddie if she fancied coming shopping with me this afternoon?"

I'm surprised by the invitation, but always up for a shopping trip and am enjoying Margaret's company. I look at James and notice that he has turned rather pale. Terry is also looking nervous and I wonder why?

"I would love to Margaret," I say smiling at her and then turn to James and say,

"You don't mind us going for an hour or so do you? It will be nice for us to get to know each other."

James swallows and says, "Why don't we have that coffee and then we can all go in an hour or so."

Strange, James hates shopping. Margaret is having none of it and says,

"Absolutely not James. I have been waiting for years to finally have some female company to go shopping with and I won't have you boys coming along and spoiling it. You go off and do your boy things and leave us to have fun on our own."

James looks resigned. "Ok if you insist, take my car Maddie and promise that you'll be careful."

What does that mean? Probably be careful of the other pride and joy in his life, his sports car. Terry looks at Margaret.

"Now don't overdo it, darling, remember we are home for a few weeks yet."

"Stop fussing and leave us to have fun," she says somewhat irritably.

"Come on, let's get the car and enjoy some retail therapy."

Poole Shopping

Margaret and I headed for the shopping centre and I could tell that she was looking forward to it. However, nothing prepared me for just how good at shopping she was. I have always prided myself on my ability to spot a bargain within a matter of seconds, but Margaret is an absolute professional.

Within no time at all, we have secured all manner of fantastic sale items and are thoroughly enjoying ourselves. Margaret is great company and I can tell that she is in her element.

"Oh Maddie," she says to me, as we browse through the sale rails of a well-known budget retailer. "You have no idea how long I have waited to be able to shop with a like-minded person. Terry is a nightmare and shadows me like an overprotective bodyguard whenever we go shopping. He thinks that you just go in, get what you came here for and go. End of. He doesn't understand that you need to look at everything, to appreciate what is a good deal when you find it."

I nod in agreement.

"You are so right Margaret. I mean, if I hadn't seen that dress I bought in the last shop a few weeks ago at full price, I would never have appreciated the fact that it's now 50% off with a further 20% on Blue

Cross. It would be wrong not to buy it. I'm sure that it'll fit once I've started my diet."

Margaret nods. "Yes, those exercise pants and top will now come in very handy. I can't believe that you don't exercise already, wasn't it lucky that we came across them in the shop-soiled rail? Now you can take up Pilates, lose a few pounds and then fit into the dress. Men just don't understand."

"There aren't many of my friends either who like to shop at the budget end," I say sadly.

"Ginge my flatmate just buys whatever she wants even at full price." Margaret looks shocked. I nod and carry on.

"Yes, it's a shame. There is nothing like the thrill of calculating how much money you have saved at the end of a successful shopping trip. I mean look at all our bags already. We have probably saved hundreds of pounds between us."

Margaret spots some trousers and a matching top on a mannequin across the aisle.

"Oh, look, Maddie, that outfit is perfect for my next cruise. We are off to the Mediterranean in a few weeks and I can just see myself promenading along the deck in that. Can you help me find it?"

"Of course, I'll take the tops section and you the trousers and we'll meet once we have found them."

It doesn't take us too long and I also manage to find her a matching scarf and a little jacket. Margaret, in turn, has found a matching handbag and three more tops along the way.

I also found three dresses and a handbag all for less than £40.

I so love budget shopping. You can re-vamp your wardrobe in no time at all and not even feel guilty about it.

We move onto the next shop happy with our purchases. Margaret points to a luggage shop.

"Let's go in there I need a new suitcase and we could use it in the meantime to wheel our purchases around."

"Good call Margaret, they have a sale on too and you could probably get a really good one in here for a great price."

I absolutely love luggage shops. They have so many different types of suitcases and bags in every colour. We spend a happy 30 minutes trying all the different ones out.

"Look, Maddie, over here," Margaret shouts excitedly.

"This whole set is half price and even has a vanity case with it. I am sure that the Union Jack Flag all over it won't matter, or do you think we could then be targets for terrorists?"

"Good point Margaret, you certainly have to think of every eventuality when travelling. It's probably best not to draw too much attention to yourselves.

There's a similar set here in lime green that would work."

"Yes, you're right of course. The neon colours are so in at the moment, aren't they?"

Just then my phone buzzes and I look at the display.

"Oh, it's James," I say to Margaret, who frowns.

"They can't leave us in peace even for a second," she says annoyed.

I answer the phone and James sounds worried.

"Maddie, are you and Mum ok? You've been gone for three hours and Dad and I were worried. He can't get through to Mum and thinks she may have turned her phone off."

Gosh, three hours! Hasn't that time flown?

"Oh, we're fine James. I'm sorry, I didn't think we had been that long."

He still sounds worried.

"Have you bought much?"

That's unlike James, he normally never even bothers to ask me what I have bought, such is his disinterest in shopping. I look at the vast array of shopping bags and realise that we have probably overdone it a bit.

"Oh just a few things, some great bargains I might add. Your Mother certainly knows her stuff." He sighs wearily.

"Maddie just remember that you have my car. It

doesn't have much of a boot and there are only two seats after all."

Suddenly I do remember and look at our purchases with alarm. He is right; this lot will never fit in.

"Sorry James I've got to go the signal is failing and I can't hear you properly, we won't be long."

"That's strange I can hear you perfectly," he says sounding surprised.

I cut the phone off and look at Margaret in consternation.

"What is it, Maddie? Are they ok?"

"Yes, they're fine, but we may have a small problem, namely the size of James's boot in the car. How on earth are we going to get this lot home?"

Margaret looks cross.

"Typical men spoiling our fun. I bet they did this on purpose. Come on let's go and see what we can fit in. Where there's a will there's a way."

We head back to the car and decide to leave the luggage for another day. Once we get to the car, I open the boot and we stare in dismay at the sight of a bag of golf clubs residing in the space, almost filling it up.

"I never knew that James played golf, did you Maddie?" says Margaret now extremely annoyed.

"No, I never did. I'm sure they weren't here when we drove down last night. I mean we had our bags in here, so how they got here is a mystery."

"Perhaps he intended on dropping them into a charity shop," Margaret says slowly.

"We could do it for him and then we would have more room for our shopping."

I'm shocked at the suggestion but understand its logic.

"Should I phone him and ask?" I say deciding that it's not our place to second guess his intentions.

Margaret looks alarmed, "Oh no dear, let's not worry him, we can find a solution I'm sure."

I look at the purchases and have an idea.

"Ok, let's get rid of all the unnecessary packaging first and then see what we're dealing with."

We start pulling things from their bags and boxes and have soon amassed quite a pile of rubbish and shrunk the amount of stuff down quite considerably.

"The next thing we can do is to wear as many things home as we can get on," I say determinedly. We have to make this work without sacrificing James's golf clubs.

We must look quite a sight as we dress ourselves in all manner of clothing. We are having such a great time and find it hilarious. I take loads of pictures of us on my phone. I never thought my first meeting with James's mother would be such fun.

We then decide to stuff as many things into the golf bag as possible and ram things into every corner that we can. We still have quite a few items though and I make Margaret sit in the car and put her seatbelt on. I then proceed to pack the surrounding items.

"I wonder if it's illegal to wind the window down and hold the carrier bags out of the window as we drive?" Margaret says thinking of a possible solution.

"Hmm, might work but it would be difficult, I mean you may drop something on the dual carriageway," I say thinking it was a good idea though.

Finally, we have fitted everything in and fill up a nearby bin with the rubbish. Luckily, it's not far from the house, so it won't be too long before we are back.

"Maddie, why don't you stop at our flat first and we can unload my shopping before we find the men?" Margaret says from behind a wall of shopping.

"Good idea Margaret, it will save us from a great deal of lecturing. I may hide some of mine there too if that's ok? I could come around later and retrieve it when the coast is clear."

"Brilliant plan," says Margaret and we laugh at our ingenuity.

Margaret & Terry's Apartment

We arrive back with no incidents to Margaret's apartment and drive into their parking space. I get out and open the passenger door and we laugh at how ridiculous we both look. Grabbing as much as we can we get the lift up to the top floor. The apartments overlook the harbour - what is it with this family, do they have to see water when they wake up? - and we soon find ourselves outside their door.

Margaret ferrets around in her bag for the key and we are giggling like schoolgirls.

Suddenly the door flies open to reveal Terry standing there looking none too pleased. James appears beside him and their faces are a picture as they take in our appearance.

I look at Margaret and she grins at me. So much for our cunning plan. The expression on their faces sends us into fits of laughter.

She pushes past them and we head inside dropping our purchases onto the shiny tiled floor of the hallway.

"Margaret! What's all this? You promised you wouldn't go mad." Terry splutters in amazement. James is silent; I think he is in shock.

"Oh, for goodness sake Terry, keep your hair on." Margaret says dismissively as though this is a normal occurrence.

"Make yourself useful and put the kettle on. James, run downstairs and bring the rest up will you there's a dear." Terry looks at James and they exchange a look of horror at the thought of still more shopping.

Margaret signals to me. "Come on Maddie, we'll go and get this lot off while the boys' sort everything out; then we can have a nice cup of tea and decide what we'll do this evening."

Trying not to look at James, I throw him the car keys and follow her into her room. She closes the door and we look at each other grinning.

"Well that ploy never worked," she said laughing.

"Oh well, they'll get over it they always do."

We strip ourselves of the many layers and stuff it all under the bed to sort out later.

As we go back into the sitting room, I wince at the volume of bags lying on the floor. It looks much more here than it did in the shopping centre.

James and his dad look annoyed, but I notice that Terry has made the tea and rustled up a plate of chocolate biscuits. We take them out onto the balcony and sit there trying to look normal.

The men come outside and join us and Terry says,

"I can't believe how much stuff you girls have bought. Did you leave any for anyone else?"

Margaret fixes him with a steely gaze and says,

"That's enough of your moaning Terry Sinclair. Don't think that I don't know whose golf clubs they were, that miraculously appeared in the boot of James's car. You were probably going to hide them away somewhere where I wouldn't see them. And as for you James, you can't talk; you seem to have a terrible property fixation and can't seem to walk past an estate agents window without planning your next purchase. You men lecture us and all we were doing was having a lovely time getting to know each other over a shopping trip and probably spent between us less than it costs to fill up James's boat with fuel for a day out. You should be ashamed of yourselves and apologise for making us feel bad."

OH, MY GOD! Margaret is a maestro at this and I am so not worthy. James and Terry look suitably chastised and she has well and truly turned the tables on them. Watch and learn Maddie, she has much to teach you!

Parkmead - Esher

James has just dropped me off after our weekend away with his parents. I am still laughing to myself over his mother. She is truly amazing, and we got on like a house on fire. We had a great time that evening and just got Fish and Chips and ate them on the harbour wall. The next day we all lazed around and went for a small trip on the boat. I enjoyed their company so much and can't wait to see them again. I'm sure there will be many good stories from their next cruise.

James didn't give me a hard time at all about the shopping and was just pleased that I got along well with his Mother. All in all, we had a fabulous time.

August 29th

I don't know where this month has gone. I have been flat out at work, organising the Ad campaign and helping Marie organise the European side of the business. She has appointed a Sales Director with experience of selling food to the Industry and he has done well securing interest for our product.

The big presentation is just three days away when the brand will be launched and trading will begin. There is to be a big presentation at the Dorchester in London, where Bellini Biscuits have invited every major supermarket buyer and organisation connected with the marketplace. We are all under pressure to make it the best launch in biscuit history and I am so nervous.

I'm staying at James's apartment in London for the next few days, so we can work through until the early hours, putting the finishing touches to the campaign and making sure that everything has been covered. Teddy is flying in tomorrow and wants a full briefing. I can't wait for it all to be over and life to get back to normal.

1st September - Bellini Biscuits European Launch

It's D Day, or in our case, Bday. Oh, that doesn't sound quite right, does it?

Note to self - never use the phrase, "B Day" in promoting the biscuit brand.

James and I got up early to make sure that we were nice and early at The Dorchester. The launch is at 12 pm, with lunch afterwards for the guests. I am so nervous and have hardly slept at all. James is also nervous and we are both on edge. Jeremy isn't nervous and keeps us both supplied with copious amounts of coffee and biscuits. I'm hoping I won't be put off biscuits for life after this, that would be a tragedy.

We meet Teddy just before the guests arrive in the room, that has been set out specifically for the occasion.

"Maddie, James, great to see you." Teddy says as he enters the room with Marie.

We smile anxiously and he laughs, still very much the relaxed Teddy that we know and love.

"Hi Teddy," I say smiling.

"Well, this is it, no turning back. I hope we have done you proud and there is not a household in Europe that doesn't have a packet of your biscuits in their cupboard by Christmas."

"That's the spirit Maddie," says Teddy, obviously pleased to think of his biscuits dominating Europe.

"Are you all set Guys?" he says suddenly looking serious. We nod and he turns to Marie saying,

"Ok, let them in. Let's do this."

The Presentation

The guests are now in place and Teddy is sitting in the front row watching the events unfold. He has been placed between the two largest supermarket buyers in the country and so is on his best behaviour and at his most disarming.

Mark, our Sales Director, Marie, James and myself are sitting in four chairs that have been set up on the stage, slightly to the side of a small podium. We each have a part to play and I feel like I am on the Apprentice.

Marie kicks off the proceedings and describes how Bellini Biscuits started and leads on to the expansion plans in Europe.

Then it is James's turn to launch the Advertising campaign. I watch him with so much pride. He is self-assured and looks very comfortable presenting the campaign. The gist of it is, there are many ways that you can eat this biscuit. There are different people in the Ad, such as a Fireman - Rob Inspired - using his as emergency biscuits - well we had to get them in somehow. There are builders who take them to work to have with their tea. Mums who decorate them and give them as treats to their children. We also have the coffee morning crowd, who arrange them stylishly on plates, while chatting with their friends. In fact, the list is endless. It's set to promote the versatility of the brand for all types of people.

James runs the TV Advert and I have to admit its genius. I can see the crowd are enjoying it and as I look over at James I feel a rush of love for him. He is so clever and has interpreted my wishes far better than I could have ever hoped.

Teddy also looks pleased, although he has seen it before today to give it his seal of approval.

James then runs through the proposed schedule, to

include TV Advertising, Posters, Billboards and Magazines. In fact, there isn't a medium that he hasn't covered and it is a very comprehensive campaign indeed.

Then it is Mark's turn to discuss the sales aspects, such as promotions, discounts and positioning in stores. He also discusses lead times and answers any questions that the guests might have.

Finally, it's down to me. Teddy asked me to close the session, and I have thought long and hard about what I should say.

As I walk up to the podium, everything I have thought of saying leaves my mind in an instant. I look out and see a sea of faces looking at me expectantly. I can see Teddy beaming at me from the front row, obviously expecting a great finish. Nervously, I look back to where the other three sit, all having played their part and delivered magnificently. James smiles at me reassuringly and I turn my attention back to the room.

"Ladies and Gentlemen." I begin shakily.

"My name is Madison Brown, and I have worked for Bellini Biscuits for just a few short months. I have been sitting over there listening to what my colleagues have said and it got me thinking. I put myself in your position and wondered why you would want to stock a new brand of biscuits in your stores? The Market is certainly already full of many types of biscuits; do you really need another one?"

I can see Teddy looking at me; not sure of where I am going with this. I look at James and he winks at me. I carry on.

"When I first met Mr Standon, it was on a flight to New York. I was working as a sales rep selling home scented products, a world away from biscuits. We got chatting about biscuits and I told him what I loved about them. It obviously got him thinking, and he offered me the job of designing the campaign to bring the brand to Europe. Like you are probably thinking now, I thought he had gone mad. Why would he trust his beloved brand to a novice? I have asked myself this same question every day ever since and it is only now that I can see why.

I am the consumer that you all need to reach. I am the person who goes into your stores and decides which biscuit to buy. Yes, there are many out there and we all have our likes and dislikes. However, I explained to Mr Standon, that if you had a good basic biscuit, it could appeal to everyone.

We all eat our biscuits in different ways and for different reasons. This campaign, as you saw, is largely based on that concept. What I have also learned, is that Mr Standon liked the fact that I was passionate about the product. We all sell things, but there are very few things that we really care deeply about. Mr Standon does care very deeply about his brand and wanted to entrust it to somebody who also cared about it as much as he did. So now you see Ladies and Gentlemen. If you decide to stock our product, you will be investing in a company that totally believes in its product. We care about the end consumer and have in fact designed the whole brand around them. You will get the full back up of a company that delivers what it promises. We will promote the product well and create awareness for the brand with the consumer. We will work with you to establish your needs and develop the brand in line with current trends and habits. I would like to thank you for your time and urge you to try our product, which you will find outside with tea and coffee. We will be around to answer any questions that you have and would also welcome any suggestions. Thank you."

As I turn to leave Teddy jumps up and rushes up to me. He hugs me and says,

"Well done Maddie. That came from the heart and I was so proud. I thank the lord that you were on my flight that day."

James also comes rushing over and hugs me.

"Well done Baby, you were great. You totally blew me away and I'm so proud of you."

Tears come into my eyes, as I finally relax for the first time in ages. This major hurdle has been reached, and the relief is enormous.

I can see Mark talking to the two supermarket buyers, who look very animated. Marie is also talking to some other buyers and there is a general buzz around the room.

James slips his hand into mine and squeezes it.

"Come on, let's get a drink and leave them to it for a minute."

We slip outside and join the other guests for a drink. Many people approach us with questions and general comments about the presentation. Most of it is very positive, and it certainly feels as though it was a success. Now we just must see how it goes down with the consumer.

15th October

I am feeling full of cold and blame the dark, damp, dismal weather. Once again, I have been working flat out and can't remember when I last had a fun time. James is away on business, but at least Ginge is home later on, so we have decided to go out for the evening with Dessie. I have tried every trick I know to get rid of this cold, but it is still hanging on.

The job is going well. The adverts have worked phenomenally and the initial delivery of Bellini Biscuits to our warehouse was sold out before it even arrived. Teddy is pleased with how it is going and we are already planning new ranges and looking at new ways to promote them.

We decide to go out for a pizza and then to a film. There's a new comedy out about a woman who inadvertently runs for President of the USA that looks good. I hope I don't sneeze my way through it though, there is nothing more annoying.

Pizza Passion - Kingston

What is there not to love about pizza? In fact, I could live on it. The Italians certainly spotted an opportunity here. We are having a great time as usual and enjoy hearing about Tommy and the Band.

Dessie suddenly looks edgy and Ginge shoots me a look as if to say - what's up with her?

"Dessie, is everything ok, you've gone really quiet?" I say to her.

She sighs and looks awkward.

"Oh, I'm sorry, is it that obvious?"

Ginge and I look at each other wondering what it can be as she is normally so chatty.

"Well I have some news, that is very exciting, but scary at the same time and I have been dreading telling you."

Wow, I wonder what it can be?

"Go on, tell us," urges Ginge looking intrigued.

"Well, Darren and I applied for a job on a Cruise ship as masseurs. More as a laugh really and to see if we could get a free holiday out of it. After a few interviews, we were both offered the job and after some training, our first Cruise is in the New Year, the 13th January to be precise."

I look at Ginge in total shock. Darren and Dessie on the high seas, rubbing their way around the world. I didn't see that coming.

Ginge recovers first and squeals excitedly.

"That's fabulous! What a great opportunity to see the world and together as well. I'm pleased for you both."

"Yes, congratulations Dessie," I say feeling a bit strange, really. I'm so used to them always being there. I recognise that something is about to change and I'm not sure that I am ready for it.

She continues to tell us all about it, but I must be in shock because I can't seem to take it in. They will be away for weeks on end and then have a short time off before the next one. Who will get our shopping now? Instantly I am ashamed of myself. I'm so selfish; of course, this is a great opportunity for them. I will just have to embrace home delivery.

We order some more wine and then it's Ginge's turn to make a confession.

"Well after your news Dessie, I think that it's a good time to tell you both my news."

I look over and note that she too is suddenly looking nervous and can't seem to look me in the eye. I have a nasty feeling that I'm not going to like what she has to say.

Dessie also looks at me with concern and I smile weakly at them, hoping it's just that she is going on holiday.

"Well like you Dessie, I have been putting this off, but realise this is the perfect opportunity. As you know, I can't be without Tommy for long and he is the same with me."

Well, tell us something we don't know. I have this

real sense of foreboding and take a gulp of wine for courage.

"Tommy has been asking me for months now to leave my job and be with him full-time. He wants me to accompany him everywhere and live with him in America."

WHAT NO?!!! I look at her, the dismay, I know very much evident on my face.

"But you can't Ginge; you can't give up your job and leave me!" I say selfishly.

"Anyway, you can't just move to another country, there are strict rules on immigration."

Ginge blushes and once again looks uneasy.

"You're right, but you see it won't matter to us, because Tommy has asked me to marry him and I will be his wife."

I can't help it and burst out crying. Ginge rushes over and hugs me.

"I'm so sorry Maddie, I have been dreading telling you. I love our life in Esher and if it wasn't for you, I would have left ages ago. Don't worry though, I will visit loads and I'm keeping the flat, you can still live there as usual."

Dessie also comes and hugs me and we must all look a sight to the other diners in the restaurant.

My world had come tumbling down over a Margarita pizza and I'm not sure if I will ever recover.

I suppose in the far reaches of my mind, I knew that this day would come. Maybe it's because of the cold that it has hit me so badly, but I feel well and truly devastated.

Ginge pours me another glass of wine and hands me a tissue from her pocket pouch.

"I am sorry Ginge, congratulations. You two are made for each other and I'm happy for you both. I'm just being selfish that's all. I can't bear the thought that I'm losing my two friends in one night and that my life is going to change forever."

They sit either side of me holding my hands. Ginge says,

"Maddie, I know this is a huge step. We are not getting married until the tour finishes in the New Year and I'm not giving up my job until then, anyway. We will all have a few months to get used to it and you can visit us as often as you like and I will be back loads to stay. Things might not actually change that much as I'm away most of the time, anyway."

I sniff. "I know, I just don't want us to drift apart. You too Dessie and Darren. It's the end of an era, just like when, Friends ended, it took us ages to get over that didn't it Ginge? She nods sympathetically.

We decide not to see the film and decide instead to head home for a night in with a DVD and chocolate. The pink panda pyjamas are needed as a matter of urgency.

16th October

Ginge has left for Rome and I'm still feeling rough. My heart is still breaking and coupled with the weather, which is awful, my mood has not improved.

It's about 7 pm and I'm sitting watching Emmerdale, in my pink panda pyjamas, feeling very sorry for myself.

I tried to cheer up for Ginge's sake and we decided that we would all celebrate her's and Dessie's news properly when she was back. I feel less like celebrating now than I did then, as the news sinks in, but I mustn't be selfish.

There is a knock on the door and I feel cross. Who on earth is it? It better not be my mum; I am not in the mood for another lecture. I rang her to tell her the news and how I was feeling and she just told me off, saying it was a pity I wasn't treading the matrimonial route like Ginge and that I needed to grow up and take control of my life like an adult and stop thinking that everything was about having fun all the time.

I drag myself over to the door and am shocked to see James standing in the doorway with armfuls of stuff. Gosh, this is unexpected and I look a right mess!

He smiles at me, that lovely smile, that always sends my heart into freefall.

"James, what are you doing here, I thought you were at work?"

He comes in and drops the stuff on the table.

"Well I left early, as I thought that you would need cheering up after your shock."

Guiltily I remember the phone call, where I totally bawled my eyes out and offloaded all my grief to him the next morning.

"I have here a selection of girly DVDs, a giant Toblerone, a box of Maltesers and some pick n mix. Two bottles of wine and my pyjamas. I thought that we could have a night in together and chill out."

I'm in shock. James doesn't even wear pyjamas!

Tears fill my eyes again and he hugs me to him.

"Don't cry Maddie, it will all work out. You still have me; I'm not going anywhere. If you want, I could stay here with you, so you're not on your own?"

This makes me cry even more. He is so lovely and I still can't believe I was so lucky that day that I met him.

He pulls me over to the settee and we just sit there together watching the rest of Emmerdale in silence.

6th November - Annual Advertising awards - The Dorchester

Tonight, James and I have come to the Dorchester for the Annual Advertising Awards. I am not here to support James as before but as a representative of Bellini Biscuits. Our television advert is up for, Best Advert, and we are both very excited.

We are sitting at a table with other nominees and Ad agencies. James is in his element and knows loads of people. He is always stopping to chat with someone or another. I, of course, don't recognise anyone but am happy to just people watch and soak it all in.

We sit at our table and I find myself next to the Managing Director of a well-known soap brand. I have a great conversation with him, as after all scented products are my speciality.

We all have a gorgeous lunch and I try to stay off the wine, but fail miserably.

The awards presentation starts and I find it interesting seeing who wins the different categories.

I am shocked, however, to see Beardy man and Ava, walk up the hallowed steps to receive an award for an advert they ran for a children's toy. Funnily enough, it was a robot. I smirk to myself thinking of Biscog. They really should cast their net a bit wider for ideas.

I look at Ava and notice that she is as frosty as ever. Beardy looks a bit tired, probably comes from juggling two identical lovers. I look over at James and he raises his eyes. I think he is well shot of Ava and smile at him lovingly.

The next award is for, Best Poster Campaign. James is nominated for this one for an Ad he ran for a sportswear brand. I note with interest that Beardy man is also nominated for this one; his Ad was for Dog Food.

The suspense is killing me and I keep everything crossed for James. If he doesn't win, then I hope neither does Beardy man. They announce the winner and to our total delight, James wins. He kisses me and goes up to receive his award. I am so proud and can't resist glancing at Ava as he picks up the award. She is looking down at her phone, looking bored. However, I know that if she wasn't bothered, she would have applauded him like everyone else. Good, I hope that she regrets her double-crossing ways.

After about 30 minutes, our nomination is called for, Best TV Advert. This is the penultimate award and I know from watching numerous awards ceremonies on television, that this must be the main one. I'm so nervous. I hope we win, not just for

Teddy, but for James. He has put a lot of effort into this and worked very hard. He deserves some recognition for his efforts.

The other Ads are also very good and I recognise them all. I'm dismayed to see my current favourite advert for toilet paper among them and hope that we can pull this off.

It seems like forever, but they finally announce the winner.

I can't quite believe it when they say, "And the award for best TV Advert goes to, JS Public Relations and Marketing, for Bellini Biscuits."

I look at James stunned. We won; I've never won anything in my life before unless you count the felt-tip pens and ruler that I won for the road safety competition in primary school. James hugs me and drags me up onto the stage with him. We hold the award aloft and James says a few words.

"Thank you for this award. It means a lot to us, as we have put so much into it. It has been a pleasure working with Bellini Biscuits and I am very proud to introduce you to Madison Brown, whose ideas were the result that you have seen tonight. She is a truly remarkable person who totally deserves this accolade. I may be biased as she is also the woman I love, but that aside I have never worked with anyone who has as vivid an imagination as hers. So, this award is for you Maddie, you totally deserve it."

I blush profusely. James said he loved me on a stage with a microphone. I have never been so happy. He beckons me over to say a few words and suddenly I feel very unsure of myself in front of these professionals. Who do I thank? What if I miss someone out? What if my top falls down like Judy Finnigan's did and I show my bra?

Oh, my God, I'm not wearing a bra!

Nervously, I approach the microphone. I look out at the sea of faces looking at me expectantly. I see Ava glowering at me, which gives me courage.

"Thank you, James, for your kind words. It is true you are biased, but then if you hadn't said those words, you would have been in trouble." The audience laugh and I carry on, warming up now.

"I would like to thank Mr Standon, the owner of Bellini Biscuits for putting his faith in us. He placed his beloved brand, in the hands of two people that he didn't know, based on his gut instinct. I hope that we have repaid his trust in us and that we continue to do so. I wouldn't have wanted to work with anyone other than James on this, as I consider him to be the best in the business, although I am biased."

The audience laugh and I finish up.

"I would also like to thank James for putting up with my vivid imagination and interpreting it so brilliantly and finally we would like to thank everyone who voted for us. We are truly grateful."

James gives me a hug and we exit the stage.

The South Bank- 11.00pm

James and I are now walking along the South Bank each one of us holding an award. We decided to walk home from the ceremony, as it is a lovely clear night.

As we walk in silence, both lost in our own thoughts, I think of how far I have come this year. I would never have thought when I made my resolutions that so many of them would have come true.

Best of all is finding James. I would never have dreamed that the man I love would turn out to be so fantastic. My thoughts turn to Ginge and with a heavy heart, I think of what is yet to come. I am happy for her and Tommy, after all, they were made for each other, but I never really thought beyond how our life is now. I am dreading her leaving, even though I can't wait for their wedding. I wonder if he will invite his parents?

I also think about how far Darren has come this year. His life has changed as much as mine and I would never have thought that he would be in the position that he is now. I'm so happy that he met Dessie and laugh to myself at the thought of the adventures they have in front of them. I will miss him too; it's like my family are leaving me behind. I sigh heavily and James looks at me with concern.

"What's the matter Maddie, are you thinking about

Ginge again?"

How does he do that? He knows what I am thinking sometimes before I even think it.

I nod. "Yes, I'm just worried life is going to change forever. I know it has to at some time, but I don't think I'm ready for it just yet."

James squeezes me.

"Things always change Maddie, that's life. Sometimes for the better and sometimes not. This is just a natural progression. Yes, it won't be the same, but things move on and it's your friendship that counts. You will find your way and your friendship is strong and will continue for many more years to come."

We carry on walking and I think back to our evening and remember the last time that we sat there at the charity auction. Then it strikes me that I never did find out what James did with his winning bid.

"James, what did you do with your trip to Necker Island, I never did ask you?"

James looks at me and smiles a secret smile.

"I was wondering when you would remember that. It's certainly taken you long enough to ask."

Gosh, was it a test? Because if it was, I must have failed miserably.

"Funnily enough, I have only just booked the trip."

"Really? When for?"

Suddenly I feel excited, but then what if I'm not invited? Maybe that's why he never mentioned it.

"Oh, am I invited?" I say worriedly.

He laughs and spins me around. We are standing by the River Thames, just like we did when he had our first date.

"Yes, of course, you are and I have also invited Ginge, Tommy, Darren and Dessie. I thought that we would all go together before they go overseas."

"Oh, James that's wonderful. You're so thoughtful. When is it?"

"Well, I hope you don't mind, but it's the week before Christmas for two weeks. Do you mind a Christmas in the Sun?"

I am stunned. Two weeks with my favourite people in the world, on a luxury Island. I launch myself at him hugging and kissing him while shouting,

"Thank you! Thank you! I love you, James. Thank you!"

Laughing, he hugs me back and all of a sudden, things don't seem as bad as they did 5 minutes ago.

Epilogue

18th December - Dublin, Ireland

The music is thumping, and the Arena is packed. Looking down from our vantage point we see Tommy and the Band giving it everything and the crowd are going wild. I look over at James and think with excitement of our holiday in just two days' time. We are all very excited and when Tommy invited us to watch the last concert before they break for Christmas, we all jumped at the chance.

What's not to love about Ireland? They certainly know how to party and in my opinion it's the perfect way to prepare us for two weeks of R&R.

My Mum wasn't pleased though. She had been so looking forward to us spending Christmas with her and Dad. I know her; she was probably hoping for an announcement from us over the Christmas Turkey. In fact, she would have fought me to the bitter end to get her hands on that wishbone.

I had to promise that we would all get together for a post-Christmas, Christmas Day, where we could pretend that it was the 25th and do everything the same.

I can see Dessie and Ginge standing over by the

window watching the concert and gyrating madly to the music and laugh to myself. I have got over my shock at them leaving me and we have pledged to meet up at least once a month for girly fun, without the men; although I'm not sure how practical this will really be.

I watch James talking to Darren. My two boys. I will miss Darren being at my beck and call. I feel like a mother watching one of her children leave the nest. At least he won't come back with his washing; they have full laundry facilities on the high seas.

Darren is also keeping the flat; after all they will need somewhere to live when they come back from their travels. I have promised to keep an eye on it for them. It will be strange being on my own, but James has told me that I can move in with him to his flat in London. I'm not sure, as I love our flat in Esher and it's so convenient for the office. Also, I don't know how many programmes on cars and gadgets that I can take on a daily basis. I like my own space to watch my endless reality programmes and soaps, while balancing a meal for one on my lap tray. It also means that when James and I do meet up, we can't keep our hands off each other and spend the whole day together. I'm worried that if we live together, it will become routine and the romance may go.

I head over to the window to be with my friends. It's too loud to talk and we just sing and dance madly. Suddenly I notice Mario flying in to deal with another pest. The Playboy Bunny is keeping him busy tonight. I look at Ginge and she nods and then nudges Dessie. Looking over at James, I signal to him that we are going to the ladies and he winks at me. If only he knew, he wouldn't be so relaxed.

Giggling like schoolgirls we dodge out of the room while Mario's back is turned and race down the stairs gripping on to our, 'Access all areas' passes.

We stop at the bottom and looking at them both I say,

"Are you sure about this? You know we're going to be in so much trouble if they find out."

Ginge and Dessie laugh wickedly and Ginge says,

"Absolutely. I've thought of nothing else since you suggested it."

Dessie agrees.

"You only live once after all and if we don't do it now, we may not get another chance."

We all high five each other and pushing the large door open we find ourselves in the main Arena and once again the noise is deafening. It's sold out, so there is not a space anywhere.

We signal to each other and split up, positioning ourselves at equal distances at the back.

I can't see them now. I'm so excited. I have never done anything like this before and have no thought at all about the consequences.

I tap the guy in front of me on the shoulder and

shout in his ear.

"Please, I need to get to the front, my friends are there, can you give me a leg up?"

He laughs and nudges his friend and between them they haul me up like a rag doll until I am high above their heads.

All at once, I am flying on a sea of bodies, across the Arena, the music throbbing around me. This is exhilarating. I feel so alive and almost can't feel anything as I am propelled forwards on a sea of hands. I don't even think about what would happen if they drop me. I'm so in the moment on a natural high and just hope that I will reach the front before the others.

We decided to have a crowd surfing race to see who would win. Ok, it was my idea, but they didn't need much persuading. Ginge will be in the most trouble if she is caught and I pray that Tommy doesn't see her coming as all hell would break loose.

I can see the stage getting closer and closer and look to see if any of the others are near me. I can't see anything but lights and sweaty bodies. People cheer as they pass me from one group to another and I think this is the best thing that I have ever done.

Soon I see the edge of the stage and I'm delivered into the waiting hands of the security men, who guard the stage like riot police. They lift me down, smiling at me, as they take in my excited look. Almost immediately I see Dessie descending on us, but no Ginge. Dessie is laughing uncontrollably and quickly we look to see if Ginge is coming. Suddenly I feel a bit anxious. It wouldn't surprise me if some guys decided to keep hold of her, but no, I see her flying through the air towards us, grinning madly.

She lands a short distance away and runs over to us. The security men usher us away from the stage area and I just have time to see Tommy's face as we run away. He looks in total shock and we dissolve into fits of laughter as we exit to the side. Tears are running down our faces and I say,

"Oh, my God Ginge, you are in so much trouble."

She holds her sides; she is laughing so much.

"I'm just surprised he carried on playing. What a professional!"

I will never forget this and we all hug each other, relieved that our mission was accomplished with no harm done. We link arms together and head off to face the music.

The End

♥

Thank you for reading The Diary of Madison Brown.

If you liked it, I would love if you could leave me a review, as I must do all my own advertising.

This is the best way to encourage new readers and I appreciate every review I can get. Please also recommend it to your friends, as word of mouth is the best form of advertising. It won't take longer than two minutes of your time, as you only need write one sentence if you want to.

Have you checked out my website? Subscribe to keep updated with any offers or new releases.

sjcrabb.com

More books by S J Crabb

The Diary of Madison Brown
My Perfect Life at Cornish Cottage
My Christmas Boyfriend
Jetsetters
More from Life
A Special Kind of Advent
Fooling in love

sjcrabb.com

Have You read?

- The Diary of Madison Brown — S J Crabb
- My Perfect Life at Cornish Cottage — S J Crabb
- My Christmas Boyfriend — S J Crabb
- More From Life? — S J Crabb

sjcrabb.com

Printed in Great Britain
by Amazon